CRITICS HAIL TRUMBO'S LAST GREAT WORK

"Wonderfully compelling reading . . . yet another piece of proof that Trumbo was a major literary talent."

—*Playboy*

"Trumbo's last work: late, great, unfinished . . . the finest work of his career. Everywhere in these brilliant pages Trumbo orchestrates a fatal antiphony of life and death."

—Edward Condren,
Los Angeles Times

"Trumbo's daring attempt to tell the story of the Holocaust not from the point of view of the victim but from that of the executioner . . . the heart of that unprecedented darkness."

—Irving Abrahamson,
Chicago Tribune

"It holds us, it appalls us, it convinces us."

—Bruce Cook,
Saturday Review

NIGHT OF THE AUROCHS

DALTON TRUMBO

EDITED AND WITH AN INTRODUCTION BY
ROBERT KIRSCH

FOREWORD BY
CLEO TRUMBO

BANTAM BOOKS
Toronto • New York • London • Sydney

NIGHT OF THE AUROCHS
A Bantam Book

PRINTING HISTORY
Viking edition published November 1979
Bantam Windstone edition / October 1981

ACKNOWLEDGMENTS

The University of North Carolina Press: From *The Works of Stefan George*, rendered into English by Olga Marx and Ernst Morwitz. University of North Carolina Studies in the Germanic Languages and Literatures, No. 78. Chapel Hill: The University of North Carolina Press, 1974, p. 375.

ISBN 0-553-13919-3

Published simultaneously in the United States and Canada

Bantam Books are published by Bantam Books, Inc. Its trademark, consisting of the words "Bantam Books" and the portrayal of a rooster, is Registered in U.S. Patent and Trademark Office and in other countries. Marca Registrada. Bantam Books, Inc., 666 Fifth Avenue, New York, New York 10103.

PRINTED IN THE UNITED STATES OF AMERICA

0 9 8 7 6 5 4 3 2 1

CONTENTS

♦ CONTENTS ♦

FOREWORD

In 1938, almost immediately after Trumbo and I were married, he started writing *Johnny Got His Gun*. I didn't know anything about writers. We had bought a small place up in the mountains. He worked all night. I watched flashes of Johnny appear at breakfast. I learned—if not about writers—about Trumbo. In order to write *Johnny*, he had to *become* Johnny.

Twenty years later, when he began to talk about writing *Grieben*, I remember saying to him, "I'm going to leave you if you're going to become this man."

Trumbo spent the early years of our marriage revealing the ultimate pain of the *victim*. He would spend the last years of our marriage exploring the ultimate evil of the *oppressor*. He was unable to finish this last novel. It remains unfinished for everyone but me—perhaps because I know what was in his heart.

He recognized the reality of evil in everyone and he was especially aware of the evil in himself. He could never accept the wholesale extermination of the Jews which took place during World War II. Neither could he ignore his human connection with it even though he was not a Jew. What he did, in fact, was to choose to take on what was not his by birth. It was his by history. It was his by a quality of conscience that would not permit him to disown it.

It was easier to become Johnny. To become Grieben meant to confront the darkest corners of his own soul.

In *Johnny Got His Gun* it was not his purpose to revel in pain. His purpose was to tell a story that might challenge the concept of the glories of war. The story said: *This happens*. The story said:

This happens because of us. In *Grieben*, it was not his purpose to revel in tales of horror. His purpose was to tell a story that might challenge the concept of evil as an external force. The story says: *This happens.* The story says: *This happens because of us.*

Had he been able to continue the novel, he meant to transcend the inhumanity of Grieben. He meant to transcend the limits of his own personality and, perhaps, even the tragedy of the era into which he was born. If he could define evil, maybe those who came after him could transform it.

He meant to bring hope.

CLEO TRUMBO

ACKNOWLEDGMENTS

First and foremost, thanks to Cleo Trumbo, who in the chaos and clutter of her move from the house she and Dalton Trumbo shared for so many years took the time to help locate materials, was unfailingly supportive and helpful, the truly great lady she is. Michael Wilson died before I could speak with him but his interviews with Bruce Cook, Trumbo's biographer, helped a great deal. Indeed, Cook's *Dalton Trumbo* published by Scribner in 1977 was most helpful in providing background on the writer. So too was *Additional Dialogue: Letters of Dalton Trumbo, 1942–1962*, edited by Helen Manfull, published by M. Evans and Company. Angus Cameron endured a long pursuit of the missing letter Trumbo had written proposing *Night of the Aurochs*. Ring Lardner, Jr., and Al Leavitt sent me in the right direction. My research associate, Linda Rolens, was, as always, crisp and insightful. Mrs. Ruth Longworth, retired State Librarian of Montana, solved some problems for me in the construction of this book. Victoria Stein added to this book through her editorial skills. Finally, Dalton Trumbo himself, whom I did not ever meet but whom I feel I know after tracing his work and life. Several times I felt he led me to the important places in his meticulous archive.

INTRODUCTION
by Robert Kirsch

The thing I am after here, the devil I am trying to catch, is that dark yearning for power that lurks in all of us, the perversion of love that is the inevitable consequence of power, the exquisite pleasures of perversion when power becomes absolute, and the dread realization that in a time when science has become the servant of politics-as-theology, it can happen again.

DALTON TRUMBO,
afternote to *Night of the Aurochs*

More than once Dalton Trumbo compared the writing of his troubling and troublesome novel, *Night of the Aurochs*, to wrestling with the devil. He knew the story would not be an easy one to write when he began it in 1960 though its premise was daring and sensational: to tell the life of an unrepentant, unregenerate Nazi, Ludwig Richard Johann Grieben, through Grieben's own words. In the end, Grieben both fascinated and repelled him, "a hero of a Satanic rather than a godly morality," yet, Trumbo went on, "by definition a hero." In a letter to Michael Wilson, he reveals his suspicions of "the idea of morality as a fact or cause." He adds, in a tone which is almost always present when he refers to the book: "Anyhow, so it goes, and so do I blunder toward the heart of this goddamned book I never should have started."

Trumbo did not complete the book by his death on September 10, 1976, though he had worked on it on and off for sixteen years. "No matter what I am working on, not a week passes that I don't get *something* written on *Aurochs* or *Grieben*, or whatever the hell it will end up being called," he wrote Wilson. To his agent Shirley Burke, in a letter written in 1976, he revealed another aspect of the work: "This is my first uninterrupted prose work in years and I am enjoying it immensely. I will, of course, enjoy it much more if it turns out to be any good."

The two views are not necessarily contradictory. Trumbo was divided about the book, aware almost from the beginning that it was the most disturbing and challenging work he had ever attempted. This in itself did not bother the author of *Johnny Got His Gun.* More upsetting was that the longer he wrote from the point of view of Grieben the more his idea of Grieben changed. The German who had started out as a representative Nazi became over the years a character Trumbo could not easily dismiss in stereotyped terms. He found it necessary to remind himself and the reader often of the horrors committed in the Nazi persecution of the Jews and in the death camps. He wanted to get to the human center of such acts.

Trumbo, the professional writer, the prolific writer, made a decision: tell the story in the first person. He had to shift that approach somewhat as you will see in these pages but he could not escape the empathy and role reversal this method demanded. Inside Grieben, he found what he also knew as a writer: that no person can be the villain of his own life. "Characters change as they are written and take on lives of their own," he writes in his afternote.

Grieben both fascinated and repelled Trumbo. A writer must energize his characters with his own experiences and emotions. It is no accident that he has given Grieben the very same operation and heart condition which he experienced, the illness which would ultimately take both his life and Grieben's. There is more than a hint that experiences in Trumbo's early life, his witness of the vindictive treatment of German-Americans in World War I, his radical hopes for a more just and equitable system in America, gave him a certain understanding of Grieben's idealistic youth.

Trumbo himself was a child of war and depression. Born in Colorado in 1905 (he thought for a time to give Grieben the same year of birth, decided to make him a veteran of World War I and moved his birth back), Trumbo came from an old American family, grandson of a frontier sheriff, son of a veteran of the Spanish-American war. Although his father had worked hard, he had little to show for his efforts and was discharged from his job as a shoe clerk because his health failed. The family moved to Southern California and Trumbo watched his father die as his family struggled for a living.

Witty, acerbic, unpredictable, Trumbo became a multi-media writer, producing four novels between 1935 and 1941, the best known of which was *Johnny Got His Gun*, and nearly forty screenplays including *Kitty Foyle*, *Our Vines Have Tender Grapes*, *Thirty Seconds Over Tokyo*, *Exodus*, *Spartacus*, *Lonely Are the Brave*, *The Fixer*, and *Papillon*. He tried playwriting, pamphleteering, and took his responsibilities as a principled citizen seriously. The contrast with Grieben is important. Trumbo was a radical of the Western Populist tradition, fought social and economic injustice, sought to help average people to fight those who sought to use, abuse, or dictate to them.

Trumbo was far from the true believer Grieben epitomized. He joined the Communist Party in the early forties, seeking the social justice it appeared to offer. But dogma and discipline went against his nature and though he became a central figure in the Hollywood Ten, the group of screenwriters imprisoned for contempt of Congress for refusing to cooperate in the hearings of the House Un-American Activities Committee, he did not consider that this was an act of heroism. He thought it nothing less than the minimum of principled action against repression and thought control.

His view was not a softening or blurring of the experience. He had paid his dues along with hundreds of blacklisted writers, actors and actresses, producers, and others in Hollywood's crafts. Trumbo was blacklisted for thirteen years, from 1947 to 1960, but managed to earn a living and to win an Oscar under the pseudonym Robert Rich for the screenplay of *The Brave One*. He was the first of the prominent blacklisted Hollywood people to win an open credit, for the film *Exodus*, and that was a turning point of the exclusionary policy. Trumbo wanted no credit for doing what he felt was his obligation as a man devoted to freedom and justice.

In *Night of the Aurochs*, Trumbo is not concerned with forgiveness or rationalization of the horrors committed by the Nazis. What he is after in this powerful and unremitting story is the notion that history, society, and ideas can victimize us and what we do to resist the victimization is the measure of our worth. The notion of *hubris* in ancient Greek tragedy is reversed. Grieben's total commitment to Nazism and German destiny is his acceptance of becoming the creature of that doctrine, which permits him to see every act as justified by the ends. His cleverness and certainty, his arrogance and affected superiority, his consistency are all evidence of his self-delusion. By making himself the total instrument of Nazi policy, Grieben believes that he has elevated himself from "a mild-looking man of no importance who shows in face and body the ravages of struggle" to a man who has lived "colossally," who has found power. What he has lost is his humanity.

Grieben's average qualities, his sense of being the mean, median, and mode of Germany, his roots implanted in aristocracy and peasantry, in contrasting regions of the country, in Protestant and Catholic religions, in the poetry, philosophy, and intellectual pursuits of German culture, in the mean and mischievous and cruel aspects of it, were intended to allow Trumbo to examine a whole range of questions about the unimaginable crimes committed by the Nazis. Trumbo wants to remind us that human beings committed those horrors, not supermen, not subhumans.

Cleo Trumbo, who knew her husband's intent, writes in her eloquent foreword: "To become Grieben meant to confront the darkest corners of his soul." She goes on to say, "he meant to transcend the inhumanity of Grieben." If necessary, Trumbo was prepared to transcend "the limits of his own personality."

Bruce Cook, Trumbo's biographer, who had read more than

one hundred pages of *Night of the Aurochs*, concluded the fragment was "more than an impressive act of literary impersonation; it is in some private sense a kind of spiritual autobiography of Trumbo, a mighty effort to understand not just a Nazi, but part of himself as well, and thus to master his own demon."

Certainly, *Night of the Aurochs* even in its imperfect state, even with its contradictions and shock, is the most important novel Trumbo ever attempted and will remain, I believe, a brave attempt to confront in fiction the human center of tyranny and unspeakable cruelty. *Johnny Got His Gun*, perhaps the most effective anti-war novel ever written in America, is a much simpler book. Trumbo's masterly techniques of ridicule and irony, his sarcasm and satire, although present in *Aurochs*, were not sufficient to encompass the horror of the holocaust. He needed to surpass his own strengths as a writer and in many respects he did.

To develop empathy with Grieben was part of this challenge. The German stood in opposition to most of what Trumbo believed in and fought for. In his life and work, Trumbo resisted victimization and dehumanization. *Aurochs* was a further expression of that impulse, the last bequest of his art and skill.

In any case, Trumbo's words speak best for himself. He completed enough of *Night of the Aurochs* (his original title, though later he toyed with the idea of calling it *Grieben*) to make the short novel, which is the main text of this book. The work consists of ten chapters, which relate the present circumstances of Grieben and the years of his early life in some detail, some bridging notes, a "diary" Grieben kept during his service with the SS extermination groups in Russia and later as commandant of Auschwitz-Birkenau, and finally, a long section which begins as a synopsis but quickly becomes a third-person narrative relating Grieben's experiences. Here we find the most shocking part of the story, his relationship with Liesel, the half-Jewish woman whom Grieben "loved," whom he had arrested and sent to the concentration camp he runs, and over whom he exercised that complete power which Trumbo began to think is at the heart of the authori-

big lump." It is not clear whether the dying Trumbo is speaking of his condition or of Grieben's.

Yet, Trumbo's voice is unmistakable when he asks himself, as the writer, the oracular question: "Is this the story of man's return to humanity?" The work itself may hold the answer.

Part I

THE TEN CHAPTERS

◆ I ◆

*I announce myself, confess my grief,
and affirm my identity with God*

I sit in my little cottage in the village of Forchheim, from which
Carolingian princes led forth the Frankish tribes to crown a German as Emperor of the Holy Roman Empire a thousand years
before the Anglo-Saxon doctrine of democracy and self-
emasculation was ever dreamed of. Here in this village I was born
seventy-three years ago and here at last, after all my wanderings, I
have resolved to announce myself. I must be heard. My last cry
must reach the world before I am choked altogether by sorrows,
before my ears burst against the thunders of chaos, before I drift,
like a drowning bird, deeply and ever more deeply into the endless
black waters of night that await us all.

I live alone in this cottage. When I go to the marketplace, I
walk alone. They speak to me as I pass, of course, but they don't
want to. Secretly they wish I had chosen some other town in
which to spend my dying years. My existence in their midst recalls
what then they pretended not to know, what now they pretend to
have forgotten.

They wish I would go away but I will not do it. I will stay in
this village until I die and I will be buried here. I will force them
to remember me and what I did and why I did it and, most especially, for whom it was done.

Loneliness is hard to bear as one grows older and I suffer from
it. But I have always suffered, as men must who try to cleanse the

world, and I have endured the pain without complaint as a decent fellow should. Even now I do not murmur except inwardly and to myself and then only of the stillness at night and the ghoulish chill of my bed. Through suffering alone have I learned better than they to understand why my fellow townsmen feel toward me as they do: I remind them of the truth about themselves and of this no man can bear reminding.

I am their unspoken folk-will, the sword they longed for, directed, and applauded. What they passively desired to do, I did. What they merely dreamed of, I achieved. What they secretly imagined, I made real. And now that everything they wanted and were given has been destroyed and made to seem unclean, they cannot endure the sight of a man, a fellow townsman, a Franconian, and a German, who delivered up his soul for them in the fiery heart of that doomed struggle.

Despite that there were excesses and even wrongs in our work, that some of our best intentions were imperfectly fulfilled, I am nonetheless completely unashamed to call myself Ludwig Richard Johann Grieben, volunteer at the age of seventeen in the 2nd Company of the 16th Bavarian Reserve Infantry Regiment, which in the last year of the first war was used as reinforcement for the 6th Bavarian Division of Crown Prince Rupprecht's Sixth Army; member at eighteen of the Freikorps; member since 1926 of the Nationalsozialistische Deutsche Arbeiterpartei; member from 1928 to 1934 of the Sturmabteilung, holding successively the ranks of Rottenfuehrer, Scharfuehrer, and Hauptscharfuehrer; in 1934 Untersturmfuehrer in the Schutzstaffel (SS Guard Unit Upper Bavaria) later incorporated into the Death's-Head Formations; SS-Obersturmbannfuehrer, Concentration Camp Dachau; SS-Hauptsturmbannfuehrer, Concentration Camp Sachsenhausen; and from 1942 until the Communists overran the installation in January 1945, SS-Sturmbannfuerhrer, Concentration Camp Auschwitz-Birkenau.

After the loss of Auschwitz we fell back slowly, distributing our prisoners among other camps along the way, trying to preserve some measure of dignity and order and morale as enemy columns thrust themselves from all sides into the bleeding heartland of the fallen Reich. When finally, on 30 April 1945, it was made known that the Fuehrer had terminated his existence in the Chancellory at Berlin, I understood at once that still another battle in the endless war for German survival had been lost and that the engagement must be broken off without further loss. Assuming civilian clothes, I filtered westward through scenes of indescribable tragedy to seek refuge in my native Bavaria in the guise of a salesman. It was there, in 1946, in the jewelled cathedral town of Bamberg, that a German, a friend of my youth, a Social Democrat who safely rode out the war years in snug protective custody at Theresienstadt, recognized and betrayed me to the Americans.

I was taken in chains to Nuremberg, and there, after the most exhausting interrogations (before a court which consisted exclusively of foreigners), I was sentenced to twenty years' imprisonment for the crime of honoring this sacred vow:

I swear by God this holy oath: that I will render unconditional obedience to the Fuehrer of the German Reich and People, Adolf Hitler, the Supreme Commander of the Armed Forces, and will be ready, as a brave soldier, to stake my life at any time for this oath.

That is the vow I took. Could any man violate it and retain one poor shred of honor? When first it was administered on 2 August 1934, did one hear objections? To the contrary! The most enlightened elements of the Anglo-American financial community approved it as making for the Reich's internal stability, and arranged their corporate relations and investment programs to correspond with the new realities it represented. Yet, only twelve years later, they were filling German prisons with German soldiers whose only crime was refusal to betray an oath which once the West itself had hailed as a guarantee of Europe's last barrier against Communism and the mongrel hordes of Pan-Slavia.

However fate decreed that I should not serve my sentence *in toto*. As sanity replaced the vengeful fury of those first postwar years and, more importantly, as our enemies in the West began to comprehend the truth of what we had told them from the beginning, my sentence was progressively diminished, first to fifteen years, and finally to six, which I served with honor.

When at last the prison doors swung open and I was conceded no longer to be an animal that must be caged, but a man at the very least, even a free man, I walked forth into the brutal landscape of a nation ravaged, occupied, laid open and prostrate to her enemies. My only son frozen to death in some Russian marsh. My daughter married through premature and brutally enforced pregnancy to an English soldier, living now in the slums of London. My wife buried on 13 February 1945 in the ruins of our German Hiroshima called Dresden to which I had sent her for safety. My pension cancelled (only since 1957, after great legal cost, has it been restored to me). My properties confiscated on order of the enemy, sold by the German state to other Germans, and the proceeds turned over to Jews.

Sick at heart, broken in health, the years bearing down on me like mountains, I came at last in 1952 back to Forchheim. I have lived here ever since. I have two stout pairs of shoes that will last the rest of my life with proper care. I have my heavy coat, a jacket, one serge suit and one to hunt in, some sweaters, my old Freikorps uniform, which no longer fits, my violin, my two guns, my walking stick, my shepherd dog Fritz, and my dying heart. Always and always this has been the story of Germany and German soldiers.

Yet I am completely resigned. When in the newspapers I read that certain Party judges, who once so generously provided our SS camps with so-called victims, now occupy positions of responsibility in the government at Bonn and in the regional governments, I feel absolutely no resentment. To the contrary, I rejoice. When I read that some good friend of SS days has been restored to rightful rank in the Army, I wish him only well. A great movement has great casualties, among which I have the honor to count myself as one. The important thing is not that so many have fallen into impotence and obscurity but that so many have been spared to carry on their work. That is why I am not bitter to see old comrades prospering while I, forgotten, live austerely here in Forchheim.

The townspeople are altogether a different matter. They belong to that bottomless cesspool of German acquiescence which accepts all and denies all, depending on which direction the wind comes from. They were happy enough to snap up Aryanized houses and shops and manufactories when they came onto the market. They danced with joy to receive perfume and silk stockings from Paris, furs from Poland, caviar and golden ikons from Russia, and Winter Relief allotments of Jewish shoes and coats and dresses and underwear and children's toys from the great assembly depots of our SS concentration camps. How do they think those luxuries were come by? They do not know. They are vague about it, just as they are vague concerning my identity and even my existence when I walk through the square on market day.

But about history, vagaries are impermissible. Although without formal education (I was engaged with life itself while my young contemporaries drowsed in lecture halls) I have always been philosophically inclined, studious by nature, and possessed of a mind which insists on penetrating to the heart of every problem, no matter how long it takes, no matter how distasteful the final truth may be. This hunger for knowledge I have nourished always on the great German classics, gladly avoiding popularizations and newsstand literature of every kind. During my six years of imprisonment I had the opportunity to devote myself exclusively to the study of history and from it I have drawn certain conclusions.

I am profoundly struck by the similarity of our present German condition to that of the American South at the termination of its resistance in 1865. There as here a homogenous people was compelled to take up arms in defense of its racial integrity. There as here the liberal ideas of Marxian-Masonic-Judeo-Christian capitalism triumphed and sought to impose by force upon the occupied nation a solution and a philosophy that could not be supported in logic. There as here the vanquished were compelled to deny their past, to stamp out the memory of all in it that was brave and glorious, and to cover with filth that which memory insisted on retaining.

Yet in the decades that followed, new generations of poets, musicians, storytellers, philosophers, and historians arose in the American South to reaffirm the glory of generously spilled blood and gallant struggle, just as will happen once more in Germany when poets begin again to sing. Today, almost a hundred years after that Civil War, young men all over the United States wear Confederate caps and fly the Confederate flag (as recently, according to *Suddeutsche Zeitung* of Munich, young men have begun to wear the swastika and affect the salute of the NSDAP). Banned at first (as in our own *Horst Wessel*), the Confederate marching song *Dixie* is greeted now with tumultuous enthusiasm wherever in America it is allowed to be played.

In all of this there is a lesson for modern Germany. The great epic of America celebrates not the victory of the North but the terrible fall of the Confederate South. The American heart thrills not to the memory of Sherman and his march to the sea nor to Grant and the siege of Vicksburg but to J. E. B. Stuart's two-thousand-saber sweep around the enemy before Richmond, to Jackson dying under the trees near Chancellorsville—yes, and to Lee at Appomattox Courthouse. Robert E. Lee. The nobility of that man in defeat. . . .

All would have been different if Hitler likewise had stood forth to surrender the German sword to masters only temporary. The sight of the Fuehrer himself delivered before that motley array of quarreling victors, robed in the terrible majesty of defeat, as serenely firm in his purpose as they were infirm, would have stirred the national soul and steeled its will in ways that only a German can understand.

He chose instead to die by his own hand in the ruins of the lost capital. This I will never cease regretting. This I will never understand. This will ever bring tears to my eyes and a knife to my throat. It was the one inconceivable error of a life stupendously lived. Perhaps the mind faltered and finally broke beneath its frightful burden. Certainly it could not have been the heart.

Ever since that incredible day I have felt myself alone and lost, even as now I am lost and alone in Forchheim: a mild-looking man of no importance who shows in face and body the ravages of struggle and who, on a day less distant than he wishes, will inconspicuously die.

Yet I have lived colossally. Everything a man can do I have done. Every emotion a man can feel I have felt. Every sorrow, every pleasure, every triumph, every defeat the heart can know has been known to mine. I have ascended the utmost peaks of ecstasy and from them glimpsed the geography of paradise. Fainting with sorrow I have stumbled through black night and the fathomless slime of deeper voids than hell itself portends. And there I have found God.

To whom is it not clear by now that God is neither good nor evil but simply All? My life is proof. God-endowed with marvelous capacities for good and evil (as are you), I used them all to the point of utter dissolution, I pursued each to its different, blinding, orgiastic end. And there stood God. And there, created in His image, stood I, no longer His likeness but His very substance, His son. As you also are His son. As you also will transform God-given capacities into action once you possess the power to do so.

The secret, as you observe, is power, and the secret of total power is oneness with God. It is not the rare phenomenon you think. There comes a moment in every man's life (if he is alert to it and understands its meaning) when complete power over *something*—a beast, a woman, even a man, and sometimes mankind—lies in his hands or the hands of his comrades like a fluttering captive bird. In that supreme instant man's power fuses with God's to become power absolute, that blinding apotheosis of divinity which no man, however base or cowardly, can reject.

Just so, when your moment of power is announced you will do as I did. Without one qualm, without a single backward glance and even with joy you will embrace power absolute, and with it the good and evil of Godhood. Either that or you will weakly acquiesce to it, as acquiesced the people here in Forchheim.

♦ 2 ♦

---

*I pay homage to those who gave me
life and commemorate their death*

My father was born one hundred and eighty kilometers south and
east of the great port of Hamburg in the town of Ludwigslust beneath the shadow of the splendid castle built there in 1772 by
Duke Frederick II. Like so many of the townspeople and nobility
of both Mecklenburgs (-Schwerin and -Strelitz) his family was of
Saxon origin, thereby differentiated from the Mecklenburg peasantry which in past times received heavy infusions of Slavic blood.
Although not of the nobility he was connected in maternal line of
descent with the family von Konneritz.

He was by nature an artist born to an age when, for the first
time in Germany, moneygrubbers and commercial parasites of all
kinds were clawing their way to power. At seven he was playing
Mozart. Through his studies in Berlin he received at twenty-three
the title of Professor. He became an immediate favorite at those
small private concerts which once characterized the social life of
the North German aristocracy.

As moneychangers started vying with *Herrenvolk* to patronize
the arts, he refused to compromise his talent to the increasing vul-
garity of popular taste and settled down as music master, first in
Munich, then in Forchheim. He played with equal skill the piano,
violin, cello, accordion, and the French horn, which he considered to be the prince of wind instruments. He taught also the

trumpet, trombone, saxophone, flute, and clarinet. He was for years Professor-Director of the *Musikkapelle* at the Gymnasium Luitpold II in Forchheim.

My mother, born Maria Caroline Bierkamp, sprang as if nourished by the soil itself from Bavarian peasant stock, dating probably from the times of Arnulf in the latter half of the ninth century. Their lands lay always in the area between Erlangen and Bamberg. Her grandfather, who held minor provincial office during the reign of Ludwig I, was murdered by socialists in the disturbances of 1847–48, from which time their fortunes steadily declined until the disasters of 1919 and 1945 finished them off altogether. The family today consists exclusively of craftsmen, clerks, and factory hands or landless peasants. Deprived of tradition, place, and history, they have surrendered not only hope but also their complete identity to the monochromatic facelessness of this antlike postwar Reich.

Through the union of these two persons—the Saxon music master Grieben from Mecklenburg and the peasant girl Bierkamp from Franconian Bavaria—I was brought into the world by midwife in my father's house in Forchheim at four minutes past midnight (my whole life has been just a breath or two after the end or before the beginning) on 9 December 1898.

It goes without explaining that my father, coming from ninety-five percent Lutheran Mecklenburg where Catholics were always regarded as clout-worthy bumpkins, was himself a Protestant; and that my mother, whose ancestors had genuflected before generations of monks, priests, feudal abbots, and regnant prince-bishops, was, not coincidentally, a Catholic.

My father, like most Northerners, had been somewhat infected with those cosmopolitan ideas which have always penetrated Germany through the mongrelized Hanseatic port of Hamburg, although the Hamburg tradition of treason and socialism was completely alien to him. As a result he cared less than perhaps he should have for communion with the State Lutheran Church and formally resigned my infant soul to the sacraments of my mother's faith. However, as I grew older, he did not fail to caution me privately from time to time against the idolatrous cunning of the cult into which I have been wetted by the priests of St. Boniface in Forchheim.

I attended mass regularly, passed through the mystical experience of communion quite unmoved, and sought the confessional as infrequently as possible. Even when trapped in the gloom of that small, crepuscular, sweat-smelling booth, I still had enough of the Mecklenburger in me to speak guardedly of private matters, sparing the priest even the smallest detail that might turn his thoughts toward a sexual life forsworn by him but radiantly opening for me. When at the age of seventeen I left my parents' house to engage with life itself, I shed all religious superstitions while still remaining nominally a Catholic. Only once again in my life did I go to confession and even that was extorted from me by the young woman who became the mother of my children. Being herself a Catholic and hence demanding Catholic rites (to which I was completely amenable and thoroughly indifferent), it was required that I be massively confessed before taking her to wife. It required almost an hour and the priest was no wiser after I left than before I came.

Not that I was an atheist or ever could be, since it is my nature to abhor all negatives. I am German to the core and no people feels so profound a sense of spirituality, of almost mystical brotherhood and mission as the Teutonic. The concept of soul in Western Europe encompasses only the individual soul, whereas a Nordic much more profoundly comprehends his soul as absorbed into and at one with the immensely vaster folk-soul of the German people—with, in short, the soul of the infinite.

Contrary to atheism, as I grew older I developed a penetrating interest in religious cults and superstitions. Some years after my departure from Forchheim and two years before the last war, I was to write in one of the highest organs of our press an analytical synthesis of Jewish with Catholic theology. It circulated in the most exalted circles and was found not to be entirely devoid of philosophical merit. During my later service at Auschwitz-Birkenau it gave me much pleasure to send to the church of St. Boniface in Forchheim a small reliquary of Saint John Chrysostom confiscated from—of all persons!—a Jewish antiquarian relocated from Salonika.

In summary, the child born under my name in Forchheim so many years ago represented in every atom of his blood and flesh and mind a perfect blend of those disparate elements that by merging make the German whole: Mecklenburg and Bavaria, North and South, Protestant and Catholic, artist and peasant, activist and dreamer, blood and soil and soul. I speak with equal fluency not only Low and High German, but also the clipped incisive speech of Prussia and the sturdy drawl of the Bavarian countryside. If there is anywhere a truer German by culture, biological heritage, geographical origins, or emotional confluence, I have not met him yet and long to do so.

My childhood was a happy one. When I reflect on it now, I realize (as always must be the case) that the security of my young years and the strong formation of my character derived exclusively from my father. He was incontestably the master of his house, as fathers to this day ought to be and aren't. Although he loved me dearly and gave many outward signs of his affection, he was nonetheless strict and demanding to the utmost. Even for minor infractions of the household rules he did not hesitate to box my ears. Serious offenses brought instant flogging. There was no arguing with him, no talking back, and no discussion of matters concerning which he had come to conclusions. Thus I was saved from those dangerous choices between folly and rectitude which youth is incapable of making without assistance. He knocked all moonshine from my head the instant it began to glow. For this I am grateful to him and revere his memory.

Unlike the women of England, who consider any form of work beneath them if there is so much as a single servingwoman in the house, my mother did all of her own cooking, using the girl only to peel and pare and measure out ingredients and clean away the waste. She did her own marketing and spent long hours rolling her special yellow Nudeln to the thinness of paper itself. Like all German brides of her class she brought to her husband an overwhelming dowry in linens and cotton goods, which she kept in an immense cabinet especially built for their storage, always redolent of cleanliness. Soiled linen she sent to the attic. So ample was my father's dowry supply that only six times a year did the laundress come to assist my mother in washing the attic's contents and refilling the cabinet once more.

The floors were washed daily, the front steps scrubbed, the bedding aired, the porcelain stove polished, the furniture dusted—and not, I assure you, with a feather-wand, which only scatters dirt and never removes it, but with clean discarded oil-dipped underwear, which in its new state absorbed filth even more effectively than in its old. Our lace curtains my mother never entrusted to a laundress, taking care of them herself: ten separate cleansings in fresh water four times each year. Each spring she went to the cleaner with her feather-quilts (*plumeaux*, we called them then in fatuous imitation of the French) and stayed the whole day while their contents were removed and cleaned and dried. Thus she made certain that my father received back into their white envelopes the same feathers he had sent, and in their original quantity.

Since internal injuries suffered at my birth prevented her from having more children, she dedicated her complete existence to son and husband. Gladly she paid to my father the same respect he required and received from his fellow townsmen, always referring to him in the presence of outsiders or even the servant girl as Herr Professor Grieben. In those days it was considered not only undignified but quite improper for a husband to open the door for his wife like a gigolo, or to allow her to precede him into a room, or to carry her parcels on the street like a servant, or to pay her other of those shallow mincing courtesies which now have become so commonplace as to lose whatever meaning was intended for them. Instead of pantomime my mother received from her husband absolute fidelity, the shelter of his solid house, sufficient allowance for nourishing food and warm clothes, the assistance of a servant girl who slept in the attic, the use of his carriage, and the dignity of his name and position.

Always at meals the platter was brought directly to my father. First he cut off the servant girl's portion and dismissed her with it to the kitchen. Then he served my mother and me and himself. No one touched fork to food until my father gave the command by taking his first bite. At the end of the meal my mother herself took the leftovers straight from table to the pantry where they were locked away to avoid pilferage. She carried the key in her apron pocket.

When at the end of his day's engagements my father wearily trod the stairway from the lower floor of the house in which his classes were conducted, my mother already had for him his slippers, his smoking jacket, his well-packed meerschaum, a pillow for his back, and his newspaper. This was her joy, her happiness complete, her life's fulfillment.

In 1943, in his sixty-third year and the thirty-fifth of his marriage, a Party member in good standing since 1938, my father while on a business trip to Munich was killed in a raid by American planes, which did not hesitate to wage a war of undisguised terror against defenseless civil inhabitants of the most beautiful city in all South Germany—a city never again to be seen by the eyes of man as once it was. From that moment forward the whole purpose and meaning of my mother's life was extinguished. She mourned him for the rest of her days. What modern woman in this whorehouse of an occupied nation called Germany can match the quality of her "new freedom" against the nobility, the sweetness, the deep profound contentment of my mother's life?

I cannot think of her to this day without recalling, while tears fill my eyes, the most beautiful lines Goethe ever wrote:

> Early a woman should learn to serve, for that is
> her calling;

Since through service alone she finally comes to
   governing,
Comes to the due command that is hers of right
   in the household
Early the sister must wait on her brother, and
   wait on her parents;
Life must be always with her a perpetual coming
   and going
Or be a lifting and carrying, making and doing
   for others.
Happy for her be she accustomed to think no way
   is too grievous,
And if the hours of the night be to her as the
   hours of the daytime;
If she find never a needle too fine, nor a labor
   too trifling;
Wholly forgetful of self, and caring but to live
   in others!

After my father's death my mother gave up our house in
Forchheim and went to live with her niece, my cousin, on a small
inherited farm property near Erlangen. I was by that time sta-
tioned at Auschwitz-Birkenau, so burdened with wartime responsibilities that I could not leave them even to pay a son's last
respects at his father's grave. Nonetheless I found time to write
each week to my mother and she to me. From her letters I perceived how impossible it was for two lone women to plough and
plant and harvest even that modest acreage, or properly to care for
the few animals that remained to them, or to cut the winter's
wood without which they must freeze. When she begged my assistance in finding deportees to keep the farm going, I did not hesitate to arrange with a good SS comrade for two Frenchmen and a
Jew (masquerading as a Pole) to be sent to Erlangen, where my
mother met and brought them to the farm.

So far as I can discover they were treated more gently than they
deserved. At the very least they were better off than in the camp

from which they had been requisitioned. They worked humane hours as prescribed by regulations and slept in the barn loft. If they did not eat luxuriously neither did anyone else in Germany in that last bitter year of our struggle. Certainly my mother and cousin had neither the strength, the desire, nor the temperament to treat them brutally.

In any event, the Jew—or the Pole or whatever they chose to call him—made such insulting suggestions to my cousin that she felt compelled to report him to the appropriate authority as required by law. The Volkssturm investigated, secured corroborative evidence, took him away with them and shot him—again as required by law.

When the Americans swarmed over Bavaria in the spring of 1945 (while I still struggled through central Germany), one of my mother's Frenchmen demonstrated that sense of gratitude that so endears his race to the world by reporting her to the occupation forces for "abusive conduct" toward the dead Jew. A full detail of occupation heroes stormed off at once to the farm, ransacked the house, and subjected my mother and cousin to the most atrocious interrogations. The sergeant in charge carried orders for my mother's arrest and removal to Erlangen. While she retired to her room to dress and pack, the Americans amused themselves with looting.

My mother did not return to them. Stunned by a world gone mad, she lay down on her bed and quietly permitted her heart to burst. The last sound to reach her dying ears mingled the crash of porcelain with bawdy shouts and rowdy songs in the coarse world-accent of the new Rome.

Thus the fate of a German wife and mother.

◆ 3 ◆

*I meet Death in the woods and swoon
to his enchantment, his cruelty, his love*

My Christian names, derived from Beethoven, Wagner, and
Bach, reveal my father's intention to make of his son a composer
or, at very least, a musician. But I was a restless, vigorous, sometimes moody lad, more given to nature's symphonics—the fluting
pipes of river, field, and forest—than those performed in concert
halls. Although I achieved a certain degree of proficiency with the
violin, and regularly played with the *Orchester-Luitpold II*, my
heart was not in it.

My marks at the *Volksschule* and later at the Gymnasium
Luitpold II were erratic. When the subject was presented in such
a way as to ignite the fires of inner vision, none of my schoolmates
could hope to surpass me. But when, as far too often was the case,
through failure of imagination my professor turned into nagging
pedagogue, I sank to mediocrity or worse, proving once more, as
already it had been proved so many times before, that truth is
more purely apprehended through submission to the soul's blinding rage to *feel* than by crafty manipulation of a halved and yel-
low-coiled slow-seeping mass of copulating worms that only
thinks.

If one bypasses altogether the so-called intellectual process and
succeeds instead emotionally to sense the inner meaning of observed reality, the edifice of truth no longer is discovered plod-

dingly and piece by piece, but instantaneously, bursting over the mind like the crash of streaming galaxies—truth entire revealed in a single ray of intuition's blazing sun. It is what we call thinking with the blood, an experience quite unknown to Western minds, which still slaver like bitches in heat for the idiot's dream of wedding Eucharist to Enlightenment.

To give but one personal example among many: Despite inclinations toward music and philosophy, I felt most at home in the world of physical action. I enjoyed gymnastics, belonged to a marching club, hiked with boys always older and stronger than myself, and loved especially to hunt. My father's belief that boys should early learn the use of firearms impelled him to give me at the age of six a smallbore single-shot rifle—a Hauserman, I think it was—and to instruct me in its use through long sessions of target practice. Until I reached the age of ten that beautiful gun was never aimed at living flesh.

But finally, as it was bound to, came the day when, gun in hand, I found myself alone in the summer forest, treading its needled paths like a ghost. The sun in its slow descent filtered great cathedral-moats of gold through latticed boughs of pine and birch and maple. It was that time of day—or afternoon—when the forest's breath, sun-stunned, yearning for night, impalpably swoons to the slow pulsations of blood and time and silence. No leaf moves. The wild pig slumbers. The fox pants softly in shadowed repose. The hare dreams at the lip of his warren. The bird makes no sound.

Suddenly the void of this tremendous silence was shattered by a squirrel whose chatter broke the peace, mocked the natural law, and ridiculed the universe. He clung firmly to a slender limb, tail whisking in glad excitement, throat swelling with imprecations, head darting from side to side to judge my reactions. His eyes, fixed brightly on mine, held no fright, no anger. Rather they ridiculed me. They were gay.

Vaguely I remember lifting the rifle in careful aim, but I have no recollection at all of pulling the trigger. I remember only the squirrel's astonishment—and mine—as gunfire crashed through the forest, ricocheted from tree to tree like a panicked stag, and then fled stuttering into distant hills until all sound died.

His first surprise cut short by still greater marvels, my squirrel seemed to turn his attention lingeringly inward, as if contemplating there a miracle, some secret revelation, a private anguish hitherto unfelt, a wonder too strange, too urgent, too poignant to be shared. Slowly his back arched like that of a languid cat. Gently his paws relaxed their hold on the bark. His dreaming body swayed toward the sun and me, and this frightened him, and for a moment he righted himself. But the dream held on. Slowly and with immense regret he surrendered to it. He fell at my feet, a small dying creature whose intentions had been misread, whose confidence had been abused.

My first feeling was bewilderment. I hadn't intended to spoil his life. I'd wanted only to train my gun on something that moved and now, in fainting submission, the victim of my curiosity lay at my feet. His eyes, already preoccupied with dying, fixed on my own a gaze so steady, so intent, so baffled, so sternly inquisitive as to make my presence above him a greater mystery than his own on the ground.

His blood and pain had no connection with me. He attributed them to God or accident or some unknown still-hidden enemy. He regarded me only as a fellow creature, perhaps even a fellow victim, chosen by fate to share with him this strange miracle of fading light and universes done to death. We stood not as huntsman and quarry but as brothers impaled together on a single shaft of pain, equally savoring its cause, its purpose, its dark repellent beauty.

Hoping to comfort him, to soothe his anxious speculations, I sank to my knees beside him. He stirred, parted his head from the earth and let it fall back again. As I drew closer it rose again, higher this time, slowly turning to the point of my approach until the small, urgently inquiring snout pointed upward to the angle of my descending face. Then, as my hand reached out to stroke him, and without forewarning of any kind, he screamed.

Startled and perhaps frightened also, I leapt to my feet. For him, at least, the mystery was solved. He had recognized the enemy. The wild despair of his cry, lingering like death in the somnolent air, yielded only to the hiss of blood in my ears and the sharp clickering of teeth as his small head pillowed itself once more against the earth.

I stepped backward to relieve his fears, but to him I was death and even my slightest movement a threat. His legs exploded to frenzy, three of them stabbing the air in mad gavotte, a single forepaw digging the earth. Mobilized by that one limb he began to pivot on his thigh, slowly and counterclockwise and always away from me, small clouds of dust ascending, harsh gasps exploding into cries.

Horror surged through my bowels. Panic marshalled its intolerable pressure behind the staring ovals of my eyes. I reloaded my gun and fired point-blank. Aimed at his head, the bullet smashed his buttocks. He pivoted no longer, but still he lived, still his forepaws clawed the air, still his eyes—those terrible eyes so filled with fear and supplication—clung to mine. I threw my rifle butt at his head and missed. I rushed in to crush his skull.

He saw the blow coming. As my bootheel descended, that frightful scream leapt forth once more, shrill as the highest note of the faintest flute in heaven, choked off at its peak by the gentler sound of small bones blending liquidly with brains and eyeballs, with blood and fur and pine needles, with earth. I snatched up my gun and ran toward the town.

When I reached home my father saw tearstains on my face and asked their cause. I told him.

He frowned for a moment and said, "But where is the squirrel?"

I told him I'd left it behind.

"Then you must go back for it," he said. "I won't have you killing things for wanton pleasure. One kills for a purpose or not at all. Find the squirrel and bring it home. It won't be properly bled but the meat's still fresh. Mama will make a soup."

I returned through twilight shadows to the forest. My squirrel lay where I'd left him, a lonely twisted, clotted little corpse, stiff as a lump of chilled pie dough, one side flat and matted with blood and crumbs of earth and sharp pine needles, the other a bas-relief of pain's distortion bejewelled with a dangling eyeball and sharp white teeth. I picked him up and carried him home. In the backyard I skinned and cleaned him by lantern light and the next day I ate him.

From that moment to this I have not with wasteful intention killed a single living creature. I have killed, of course, but always for food or for a social purpose higher than my own desires. As further penance for the sufferings of my little squirrel, I have never since pulled a trigger without the certainty of a clean kill.

Many years later, when I, with others, was privileged to be invited by His Excellency, the Reichsmarschall and General-feld-marschall Hermann Goering (acting in his capacity of Chief Forester of the Reich and Master of the German Hunt) to shoot at Karinhall, his country estate in Brandenburg near Berlin, I brought down two stags and an aurochs the first day out, and only one of them required to be given the *coup de grâce*. Their meat was donated to an orphanage for the children of German soldiers fallen in battle.

Still later, in the midst of a spiritual crisis of the most appalling nature, the memory of that small horror in the forests of my youth opened my mind to fresh apprehensions of truth without which I could not have retained my sanity. Recalling how at first the squirrel lay at my feet so serenely devoid of fear, dying placidly because quite unaware of death, equally unaware of himself as victim as of me as killer, I came to understand that any life is more painful than any death; that fear of death is worse than death himself; that death-fears come only when the face of death is revealed; that he who conceals death's presence and speeds him swiftly to his target partakes of the nature of God's own mercy.

So much for killing when one has to kill. It's a lesson which sooner or later all men must learn. There exists on this earth no government which does not command the killing of human beings as the citizen's first duty in time of war, or as a matter of legal justice in those brief intervals between wars which, for want of a better word, we call peace.

For the latter, I will only say I thank God that in today's truncated German state no gas chambers operate and strict laws forbid the killing of people by any means in any circumstances, although it is well known that American gas chambers are public institutions, fiercely defended by popular opinion, and generously used. So much for changing times. So much for humane killing. I mention this in hatred of no one.

There is still another kind of killing which broods in those shadowy borderlands of the human heart where everything becomes its opposite in that slow-circling moment when darkness covers sin and the blood turns hot and thick and deadly. My first experience of it came not long after my murdered squirrel; in my second, after it had lain dormant for years, it sprang up like a wakened beast to consummate that welter of pain and foulness which was my middle-life. I speak of an urge to kill which comes in tenderness and terror from a lover's passion to absorb the beloved to the last drop of her juices, to the last atom of her flesh, to the last faint suspiration of her spirit's breath; an ecstasy of desire so pure, so poignant, so irresistible that the adored can be taken only through passion's apotheosis when blood stings the tongue like a whip and pity dies and pleas change to sobs and sobs to a sigh, and her life flows silently into yours, and all that was corruptible in her then belongs to death.

What is it in us that makes us cruel when we long to be kind? Where is that point of no return at which caresses become torment and love's satiety shrieks for death? Why is the good in us so fatally bound to evil, and why in the end does evil always triumph? For it does. I have seen it. As inevitably as the equinoctial processions good turns to evil, desire to lust, love to hatred, life to death. Why is the exception so cruelly hidden from us? Or is there no exception? I, who searched so long, have found none at all, nor have I ever known the man who did. There is something wrong in the world. Dark days, black nights, and the endless singing of loss in the blood. . . .

♦ 4 ♦

I inhale the summer perfume of Inge's loins and am driven by it to murder

Next door to my father's house, separated from it only by the width of a narrow brick wall, stood the Kulig house, identical with our own. Herr Kulig was a notary and grain broker whose tireless wife had presented him with an unbroken sequence of daughters. How many there were in all I cannot now remember, although certainly there were six or seven at the very least. The one who most captivated my childhood dreams was little Inge.

I don't precisely recall how old she was when the event, which now concerns me, happened. Since I was twelve, she must have been ten at least, possibly even eleven. As I peer at her now through mists that have drifted far in fifty years or more, she seems small for her age and quintessentially feminine, with straw-colored hair and ice-blue eyes and slim black-stockinged nettle-catching little legs. More than anything else I remember her smell: an odor so delicately acrid of musk, so modest, so humid, so challenging that even now its evocation tightens my breath and speeds the flow of my blood—vain tribute to those surging storms of unrequited sensuality which once emanated from her small person as naturally as thunderbolts from Jove.

It was one of those hot, glaring summer afternoons at the tag of a three-day foehn when anything can happen. Inge and I sat together on the grass in the shade of her house, protected from spying eyes by a thick hedge of laurel. We were engaged in that one childhood game which is never undertaken innocently, and particularly not by a lad approaching thirteen: We were playing house. As father and mother we sat absorbed in the task of persuading our children to nap quietly beneath doll quilts in their separate beds.

Inge's child was a tom kitten, mine a new-weaned doe rabbit given to me by my mother's sister. She was the most beautiful rabbit I'd ever seen, a soft pulsing bundle of white fur topped by a jaunty grenadier's cockade of golden seal-brown ears. I loved her more than any pet I'd had before, and, now that I think of it, more than any since.

Cats being sensuous by nature and easily seduced with caresses, Inge had greater success with her kitten than I with my rabbit. By and large, her child lay resignedly on its side, head against pillow, thoroughly tucked inside its quilt, giving small trouble aside from an occasional wail against the unnatural warmth of its situation or, when it sensed a lapse of Inge's vigilance, a savage lunge, after which it was instantly retrieved, admonished, stroked, hypnotized, and returned to its downy womb.

My rabbit was a different matter. She considered it unnatural to lie on her side like a cat, while the mere touch of quilt to her back, triggering instinctual fears of enemies that pounce, threw her into paroxysms of struggle. Sheer exhaustion occasionally forced her to yield for a few seconds and lie quietly, her lovely brown ears limp against the pillow, her eyes gigantic and luminous with appeal. But the instant her strength returned she sprang to her feet and leapt from the bed in a movement swifter than my hand could match. That I recaptured her each time did not in any way diminish her expectations of ultimate escape.

While laboring to control our beastly offspring we grumbled against them monotonously, as parents will. This one had wet her panties, shame-shame, the other had defiled himself even more shockingly; this one had been caught with a nasty word on her lips, that one had peeked on his mother while she lay in her bath. Thus we sat, thigh to hot thigh, voicing patient desperation as their conduct, passing from lewd to obscene, approached the fetid brink of sheer depravity. Where have they heard such language, we asked, how can they even imagine these things, much less commit them openly before our eyes? What can we do but spank them? We spanked gently, however, not wishing to inhibit them completely from carnal appetites. I suggested that father spank mother, and vice versa if necessary, as atonement by example for the children's indecencies, but Inge objected. Mothers never spanked fathers, she explained, and could not themselves be spanked by fathers in front of their children. She would have none of it.

Each time she shifted position to care for her child, small puffs of air escaped her pinafore—exhalations warm and rich from the summer hollows of her body, sweet with the marshy tang of sweat and skin and femininity. She infused the whole world with her fragrance. Visions and mysteries drifted like clouds from her presence; fantasies shimmered fivefold at each turn of her thousand horizons; the very universe swooned to the spell of her sun-distilled essence, turned languid, drowsed sweetly, dreamed.

"Ing-*eh!*"

From the back stoop a mother's voice summoned her child to food. I put my hand on her knee and begged her not to answer. We would run away, we would hide for a while, we would play delicious games where no one could see us, we would touch each other in secret places, concealing nothing, discovering all. For a long moment she appeared to listen, her eyes dreaming the words as I whispered them. Then, with a smile that fell between regret and mockery, she gave a prim shake of her head and rose to her feet. Fiercely I clasped her small unfleshed hips in my arms. She turned against the embrace. The salt of her thigh touched my tongue. I pressed a cheek where tongue had tasted. We locked in silent, undulating struggle, she on her feet, I on my knees. In the midst of this, Frau Kulig's voice called again. Inge twisted, laughed softly, squirted from my arms like a fish, flashed to the corner, and disappeared.

I was alone. I was lost, forsaken, abandoned, a burning point of desolation marooned forever in the boundless immensity and breathless silence of summer. In the circle of my arms where Inge had stood, there now lingered only quiet air which had been intimate with her and still carried the taste of her skin.

How long I knelt in that posture of prayer I do not know and what happened thereafter I cannot explain. I do not excuse myself for it. I cannot apologize for it. I cannot understand it. I do not like it and I did not like it then. Nonetheless it happened. I write it here because it is the truth, and truth at this age in my life is more important than anything else. It must be faced up to and admitted if it is ever to be understood. I feel time running away with me, carrying me off to far places without my consent. I must leave everything behind, the bad as well as the good; all must be declared and sworn to, even though not explained.

A sound so soft I couldn't be sure I heard it broke the enchantment. I turned. My little doe again had leapt for freedom. I sprang to my feet and rushed her. One slave had escaped, the second would not so easily thwart my love. I pounced harder than I'd intended to. The impact against shocked lungs burst deep in her throat as a squeal, instantly choked by her gulping need for air.

I picked her up and buried my face in her belly, slowly exhaling warm breath against her skin to soothe her, to convince her of loving intentions. Then I returned her to the bed, nestled her into it, turned her again on her side. Before drawing the quilt I petted her from brow to tips of hindpaws in long, lingering, gentle strokes. She gave no sign of acceptance. My caresses turned heavier, pressing her against the mattress, mesmerizing her, as I hoped, to a state of weariness so profound that she would lie quietly at last and fall asleep.

She sighed in apparent resignation. Her eyes drooped. I continued stroking her, confident now that she liked it. Perhaps I pressed too hard. Perhaps her passivity was merely feigned. I did not feel the subtle contractions her body—those secret marshallings of tensile energies hitherto reserved—until they exploded against the pressure of my hand. With the speed of a single gasp she flipped in the air, stiffened, and came down on all fours to face me, flanks quivering like a nervous colt's, pink nose-tip signaling her heart's alarm—a tiny metronome gone wild in beating out the broken, mindless rhythms of mindless terror.

I caught her as she leapt again. Securing her forepaws in my right hand, her hinder in my left, I lay her in the bed once more on her side. And then, her paws still in my grip, I began slowly to stretch her body end against yielding end. Her head arched backward until the gold-brown ears drooped limp against her spine. She gasped for breath. I diminished the pressure. Relief only galvanized her to new frenzies, wilder and fiercer than all which had gone before. I began once more to draw her extremities against each other.

Her head and ears sank again to her spine. Slowly, madly she permitted her body to grow longer, leaner, less resisting, released her rib case to plunge forward as her belly sank to a crescent, summoned her lungs to thunder against her palpitant heart as each struggled to fulfill a function without which the other could not live. Only a little more, I felt; only a few more seconds and drowsiness would come. I pleaded softly with her: she must stretch, she must relax, she must grow languid and drowse, she must sleep.

She stiffened in spasm. Her head plunged farther back, farther and still farther, twisting slowly until one temple strained flat against her haunch in a position that directed her stunned eyes full at my face. Her mouth flew open, wide and pink and trembling; her lungs strained convulsively to expel the last pocket of breath still trapped in them; her throat quivered against the lingering passage of a sigh that held in its heart a memory of lost infants mewling in chorus through distances unknown and time unmeasured—a sigh of intolerably sweet relief which went on and on and on and did not stop until her body turned limp in my hands.

I knew what had happened, but admission even to myself

would have been too frightful to endure. I pretended not to understand at all. Above the roar of storms and the crash of thunders at the horizon of my unconscious I heard the sustained vibrato of an E-string plucked or broken—a single note, high and fine as spun glass, lingering in my ears only as a sustained resonance that grew fainter, higher, sweeter until it died on those dark incoming tides of lethargy and torpor and regret that bore me at last to nepenthe and the golden lassitudes of absolution.

Moving now in a trance I placed my little doe once again on the bed she had so tragically refused. This time she yielded. I smoothed her pale head against its pillow. I stroked her limp, golden, seal-brown ears. I drew up the covers, kissed her brow in farewell, turned silently away, and fled on tiptoes to my parents' house. I entered the front door unseen, crept past my father's studio-rooms (a student was tuning the E-string to insecure flats and sharps—he had no sense of pitch), slipped up the stairs and into the cool shadows of my room.

I disposed myself on my cot with all the care of a clerk at inventory making sure each part of the whole is complete, undamaged, in proper relation to all others. Cautiously I relieved my lungs of stale air (I have always held my breath in moments of stress or expectancy) and filled them with fresh, repeating the action slowly, regularly. Once their natural rhythm had been restored I lay still, entirely composed, waiting for the sound I knew must come, the bell that would toll my loss and proclaim my innocence.

Silence merged with time, and time with life. Sounds from the kitchen below, sounds from the bleak fiddle of that wretched student, sounds of my father's voice in anger and reproach, sounds of a dray lumbering the afternoon street, sounds of beams and walls and timbers relaxing against each other, sounds of shadows in slow retreat from the sun. I lay perfectly still, allowing no muscle to move. Although filled with the most delicious languor, my consciousness still remained alert, expectant.

Then it came—a wild clamor below, staccato of small feet

drumming the stairs, crash of door thrown open, image of Inge proclaiming tragedy.

I jumped from my cot. I ran from that room, ran down those stairs, ran out of that house, ran across that garden space through clattering gates, ran to that other house and there, behind that other hedge, I knelt at last before the bier of murdered love. Only then could I weep as I've wept ever since in my dreams, as I know I shall weep in the hour of my death, and through it, and beyond it. Tears for the beauty of life while it lives; for its loss when it leaves; for the guilt of those left behind, unloved, untaken by death.

How does a bird feel when it dies? A fish, a bug . . . the infinite worm?

I think it weeps.

♦ 5 ♦

"It was the just and vengeful sorrow
of Frija for the murder of Balder,
her son, that drowned Valhalla's
golden towers in the blood of dying
gods and filled the world with darkness"

When I wasn't dreaming of Inge and the perfume she exuded into the motionless summer air, and that incredible instant when I had clasped her hips and touched my tongue for the barest instant to the salt-sweet taste of her skin, I spent most of my time with Gunther Blobel, who was my best friend. He was a tall, slim lad with blue eyes and the gentlest smile I have ever seen. He was the only son of Herr Heinrich Blobel, the undertaker.

With the exception of Count Firsky, who was ninety-three and slowly liquefying with age, Herr Blobel was reputed to be the richest man in Forchheim. This was only natural, since he dealt in a universal necessity, and there was no way to avoid availing oneself of his services without moving bag and baggage out of his jurisdiction into the territory of some other "mortician"—a word just coming into use—and there was none closer than Bamberg or Erlangen.

Herr Blobel's display rooms fronted on the Wilhelmstrasse across from the Rathaus. Here, through black velvet-draped plate-glass windows, he displayed four rows of coffins to the public, the upper half of each coffin propped open to reveal the comforts available within. Artificial wreaths of roses and lilies hung from the walls between gleaming, gold-framed, oval porcelains of the Madonna and somber-hued crucifixion scenes with halos which began waist-high and continued, through whole flights of bugle-blowing cherubim, to the intensely blue vault of heaven and the angry rays of a newly risen sun.

Because it was Herr Blobel's hope that Gunther one day would take charge of the business as his own, it pleased him to give both Gunther and me full run of the place. Thus it was not at all unusual for us to see some of the most prominent citizens of Forchheim lying quite naked on the table to which Herr Blobel had assigned them to "drain" on while Herr Blobel chipped away outside at his gravestones.

The tables themselves had been devised and installed eleven years earlier by Herr Blobel himself when he purchased the establishment after its original owner was sentenced to prison for gutting his clients, stuffing them with old newspapers, sewing them up again, and selling their accumulated entrails to a few favored peasants as pig feed. It was considered one of the worst scandals in Germany until shortly after the war—1922, I think it was—when a butcher was arrested for slaughtering and rendering nineteen young German boys into sausages. There were, however, certain differences. Thanks to the Allied Occupation, Germany was starving to death in 1922, and the murderer was not Bavarian but Silesian.

Nonetheless, as Herr Blobel used to say, "Dead meat attracts rats," and it was quite impossible to keep the embalming room entirely clear of decaying flesh fragments. Herr Blobel therefore kept a large half-starved female cat named Frija locked in the embalming room all night long. He gave her nothing to eat or drink aside from a bowl of water, and she repaid him with scores of dead rats, mice, lost birds, and an occasional squirrel. Each time she littered, Gunther and I stuffed her kittens into a burlap bag and drowned them in a drainage ditch less than a kilometer from town.

Most of the coffins in Herr Blobel's showroom were of wood, the cheapest being gray, fabric-covered pine. The better ones were made from carved walnut or mahogany with polished brass handles and the deceased's monogram carved to order. The finest of them all, which Herr Blobel always referred to as a "casket" rather than a "coffin," was of solid bronze with a trio of Corinthian pillars at each corner, heavy loops of purple silk velvet swinging from handle to handle, and seals which provided a "fifty-year guarantee against seepage of any kind."

Opposite the coffins, mahogany doors concealed the wardrobe department, which, in terms of profits, stood second only to the coffin division. The Germans being a thrifty race, one would have thought them too canny to buy new clothes in which to be buried, but Herr Blobel had a flair for selling shrouds which amounted almost to genius: The deceased's present wardrobe was far too fine to be shut away for all time. It had a sentimental value that, were it disposed of in the moment's wild grief, could later result in bitter regrets. Tailored of the finest wool and lined with material of a quality almost impossible to be obtained in these later days, its gift to St. Boniface as a charity would bring down innumerable blessings upon the head of its donor.

In view of the fact that not only the deceased's nearest and dearest would be present to view the remains, one should remember that present and former business associates as well as current creditors, if any, would also wish to pay tribute to one who had led so exemplary a life. In view of all this might it not be wiser if the deceased's clothing were disposed of later, thus allowing time for thought unsullied by emotion and calculations uninterrupted by the moment's immediate demands? Might it not, in short, be the better part of wisdom, as well as a last and most graceful tribute, to clothe the deceased in a tailored shroud, handmade throughout (as confirmed by the Royal Coat of Arms on the inside cuff of each garment) by the firm which performed the same sacred service for the House of Wittelsbach? Who but a Prussian could refuse?

Or—and here the gears shifted very cunningly—the material *had* turned a bit shiny over the years, didn't one think? The slight fraying of the left jacket cuff could, of course, be concealed, but what was one to do about that portion—small, to be sure, but nonetheless there—of the lapel which apparently had been slightly burned, from the dottle of a pipe no doubt, and then rewoven?

Once begrudging and sometimes even grateful consent had been obtained, Herr Blobel flung the wardrobe cabinet doors open and launched into a complicated discourse on the advantages of what he called the "unitary shroud" to those who had "entered the dreamless land of eternal sleep."

Shrouds for the men consisted of a necktie, waistcoat, jacket, and trousers to the knee, tailored as a unit so that all one had to do was thrust the deceased's arms into the sleeves, slip the cadaver onto its belly, and achieve a perfect fit by the use of safety pins or, occasionally, a needle and thread. Underwear was considered unnecessary, although socks and stockings sometimes completed the ensemble. For gentlemen there were, in addition to a bountiful selection of military uniforms, business suits of varying quality: black morning coats with discreet gray cravats, dinner jackets with white pocket-handkerchiefs, and even what could have been considered white tie and tail ensembles, were the tails not so short.

Voluminous white silk evening gowns trimmed with lace and touched up here and there with artificial baby rosebuds or sprigs of edelweiss dominated the ladies' wardrobe section. Lavender was the favorite color after white, followed by melancholy grays and dismal blues. No female underclothing of any kind was visible except for white stockings and gloves. Here again safety pins made it possible for the basic "unity shroud" to fit any female cadaver from the truly mastodonic to those withered gaunt by age or underdeveloped for lack of it.

The remarkable thing about Herr Blobel's way of showing his shrouds for either sex was his ability to display the garment from every possible angle without permitting his customer so much as a glimpse of the safety pins and hooks and clamps and cords and laces which constituted the "unitary shroud" and ultimately caused their manufacturer to take over the name as a trade title.

A beautifully carved door with a "Please Do Not Enter" sign in gold leaf led one to the working heart of the establishment: the embalming room itself with four slanted glass tables (each with its own water faucet), shelves of bottles, rows of buckets, racks of cutlery, cans and cups and bowls, small suction and large injection pumps, sewing equipment and, in one corner, a makeup department with tables containing dyes, waxes, creams, acids, blemish removers, small scalpels, cotton wigs, malleable skin hardeners, new eyelashes, rows of gleaming white front teeth, nose and ear plugs, crosses for folded hands, and the like.

The embalming room gave onto an open work area at the rear of the property, where Herr Blobel added to his already substantial income by carving gravestones. He made no pretension to sculpture, but if you wanted your name and dates and a scriptural quotation of reasonable length—no virgins, no cherubim, no crucifixes—Herr Blobel could give you a legible job at a legitimate price.

The embalming room was rarely full, but neither was it often completely empty. Thus, through an incredible piece of good luck, Gunther and I chanced to be in it on the day old Count Firsky unwillingly surrendered his fortune to a mad nephew, who had been confined to an asylum for over two decades, and his soul to God.

When the word came through, Herr Blobel was in such a lather of excitement that if one were not privy to the almost inhuman efficiency with which he not only confronted but overwhelmed any form of crisis, one would have thought him quite mad. He dispatched Kapitzan, his man of all work, to the desolate ruin called Schloss Vauden, which Firsky had inherited from his niece, who was related in some irresponsible way to the last grand duke of Cassel, with orders to seize the count's remains and transport them to Forchheim before a swarm of notaries, grand ducal tax snoops, and starving creditors (of whom the count was reported to have an incredible number) had a chance to sink their incisors into what remained (if any) of the old man's assets.

After Kapitzan had hitched a team, tossed a stretcher onto a canvas-covered flat-back wagon, and set off at a gallop, Herr Blobel turned to me. "And you, Ludwig!" I jumped as if I'd been shot. "You run across to Herr Brinkerhoff's shop. Tell him to come at once. I want every sealing device on that bronze casket checked out. I don't guarantee against leakage for fifty years without making certain everything is in order."

"Yes, sir!"

As I started out of the embalming room, Herr Blobel turned to Gunther. "Gunther, you go find your mama. Tell her she must come here at once. Tell her that Count Firsky, God rest his soul, is dead and on his way this moment to the embalming rooms! Tell her I've been holding that bronze waterproof casket with Firsky in mind for eleven years—no, no, don't bother her with that, she knows it already. Tell her as briefly as you can that Firsky is no longer with us, and the lining of his casket needs cleaning. Including the pillows, whose stuffing I'm sure she realizes is sixteen percent pure eiderdown! While she cleans the fabric, you two will polish. Wheel it back here so idlers can't watch you at your work, supply yourselves with all the rags and fluid you need, and *polish*. When you're through I want that casket so slick and shiny that a bull blowfly can't land on it without sliding off the other side. Am I clear?"

When Gunther and I returned, Herr Kapitzan's lathered horses were just backing the rear of the wagon up to the embalming room door. Herr Blobel strode to the wagon before it came to full halt and threw back the canvas cover beneath which Count Firsky lay strapped to an army cot. After the most cursory inspection, as if to make certain he'd got what he'd bargained for, he thrust both count and cot under his right arm and strode with his booty through the open garden of headstones into the embalming room.

Once inside, Herr Blobel swiftly untied the count from his cot, tossed the cot aside, and addressed his attention to the deceased, whose nightshirt had hiked well above his navel, leaving exposed a knobbed arthritic complex of meatless bones crouched into the vaguely defensive foetal position of a beleaguered infant.

Clearly the first problem was to straighten the body from its triangular position to one more suggestive of peaceful rest after a task well and faithfully performed. To accomplish this, Herr Blobel with one hand held the count on his back, as one would an obstreperous child, while the other swung a 5-liter bottle of distilled water from the floor at the head of the table, as effortlessly as if it were a teacup, and deposited it firmly in the hollow of the count's sunken belly.

With his client thus immobilized, Herr Blobel then addressed himself to the task of straightening the twisted corpse into the general shape of a human being. Over the years the count's arms had almost fused to his rib case, with the result that it required considerable effort even for Herr Blobel to separate the arms and secure them by stout cord to the sides of the table, thus exposing a pair of hairless hollows which once had been armpits.

Next, with the precision of a man who not only knows his work but actively enjoys it, he moved to the foot of the table where, with considerably less effort, he spread the ancient legs as far as the crotch would permit, thus removing from the inner thighs their only protection. Once the old man's ankles were secured by cord to the sides of the table, Count Firsky's posture was cadet-straight and so slimmed by attenuation (his breast bones cast shadows) that he looked like some extremely well-preserved specimen from an archeological dig.

Rolling a special apparatus to the head of the bed, Herr Blobel removed the 5-liter bottle from the count's belly, suspended it from the apparatus directly above his client's head, and plugged it with a stopper from which extended a rubber tube equipped with a clamp valve for volume control.

From this time forward I began to detect in Herr Blobel a subtle change which affected every movement he made, and yet of which I think he himself was not at all aware. It would have been quite wrong to call him possessed as he approached the climax of his task, but it would have been equally wrong to describe his attitude as no more unusual than that of an efficient workman calmly fulfilling the conventional requirements of an ordinary job.

I first noticed it when, without being immediately aware of the change, I realized that the tempo of his work was turning imperceptibly faster. Then, bit by bit, his eyes grew brighter; the play of his long fingers turned more delicate and yet somehow stronger; the certainty of his movements became almost choreographed; the set of his lips grew stern with concentration; his cheeks fairly glowed with the satisfaction of a man who has set for himself an impossible task and is handling it on even terms. During the entire period he spoke not a single word to Frau Blobel, who was working on the coffin's luxurious slumber arrangements, nor to Gunther nor to me, who were half-dissolved in sweat and cleaning acids.

He then rushed to a jar filled with water or disinfectant in which half a dozen scalpels of varying sizes stood soaking, handles up. Rejecting four of them as unfit for his purpose, he seized a fifth, tested its blade against the horny hide of his thumb, grunted with satisfaction, and set to work.

Two deep right and left slashes on each side of the groin started a flow of blood which he observed critically for a moment before swooping to the head of the table where the addition of two four-centimeter slashes—one under each armpit—added substantially to the flow he desired.

Then, in a gesture that would have done credit to a prestidigitator, his scalpel struck the carotid artery like a cobra, splitting it open for at least three centimeters. Into this slot he inserted perhaps two centimeters of rubber tubing from the bottle suspended overhead, released the snap valve, and turned the water faucet at the head of the table to a moderate flow.

In an instant, water-thinned blood began almost melodiously to trickle through glass gutters on each side of the table into the sewer opening at its lower end. Old Count Firsky's body seemed visibly to shrink while his bones grew larger and the transparent skin he had brought with him turned a dirty-cotton gray.

Thus began the process which would transform a ninety-three-year-old gnome into a uniformed courtier of the Grand Duchy of Cassel, painted down to sixty-five and capable of leading the march-by of a full regiment at dress attention.

"They say he hasn't eaten for five days, thank God," said Herr Blobel to his wife, "so a thorough flushing will do the job."

"Poor man," said Frau Blobel, digging into the lower end of the bronze casket for the last of its accoutrements.

"Well, we all must go *sometime*," said Herr Blobel. "When I bought that casket the doctors gave him six months. Instead he has kept my capital tied up for eleven years. When you're finished there, mix up four liters of Hauptmeyer's Gum Paste Number Four, and see if you can't . . ."

At this point Frau Blobel gave a violent start and snatched her hand from the coffin as if it had touched a live wire. "Oh my God," she cried, "it's Frija!"

Herr Blobel whirled on her. "What do you mean, 'Oh my God, it's Frija'?" he demanded.

"She's littered again," quavered Frau Blobel, almost in tears. "She's littered at the foot end of Count Firsky's casket!"

"Oh my God!" Herr Blobel rushed to the casket, bent down, and peered inside. "It's too dark," he said, "I can't see." Then, as he rose, "Of all the caskets she could have hit on . . ."

"It's the quality," Frau Blobel suggested somewhat timidly.

"The casket's been here eleven years," shouted Herr Blobel, "why should she begin to prefer quality *now*? Oh well." He turned toward the rear door and the gravestones beyond it. "Clean the mess up and sprinkle it with toilet water. *Soak* it in the stuff. You there!" he was talking to Gunther and me now, "you boys sack the kittens when you've finished polishing and get rid of them. We'd better feed the cat for a day or two until she gets back her strength. Otherwise we'll be overrun with rats."

Thoroughly enraged, he overdosed his wife's arm with a solu-

tion so powerful that it brought tears to her eyes, after which he
bound it with cheesecloth tied in a double-bow knot.

"It's too tight," said Frau Blobel, "it hurts."

"Tight at first," he said calmly, returning to his work, "and
looser afterwards. Half of the tightness now is imaginary because
it's the first time you've worn such a bandage. Don't forget to wet
the inside of that casket with rose water. By morning the whole
place will smell like roses."

"Lilies," corrected Frau Blobel.

"Roses!" repeated Herr Blobel, raising his voice.

While they argued about scents, I confined the squirming kittens to the small soiled pillow on which they had been delivered.
Gunther, pinioning Frija's forelegs, held her snarling mouth and
bared teeth close to one of the glass gutters that started Count
Firsky's water-thinned blood on its long journey to the sewer
system.

Without even a precautionary sniff, Frija dipped her tongue
into the last blood of the last Firsky and lapped it up as fast as it
came, pausing only to catch her breath and try for a nip at the old
man's throat which, she smartly concluded, was the source of
such exotic fare. After we felt she'd had as much as time would
permit, we thrust her and her offspring into a small wooden pack-
ing box with plenty of air holes and hid it outside behind a slab of
gray limestone while Frau Blobel, thoroughly out of patience,
continued the argument with her husband.

"I tell you we do not *have* any rose water," she said firmly.
"We have only essence of lilies. We used all of the rose water
when Fräulein Grossfeld threw up while that photographer was
trying to raise her head high enough in the coffin to get her pearl
choker into the picture."

Herr Blobel thought for a moment, his face turning darker as
memory stirred. "You are right!" he said, fiercely brandishing a
stomach pump at her. "I remember it all now, and especially that
fool of a photographer! And then the minute I got the mess

cleaned up they took the choker anyhow! They weren't going to bury *that!* No, *sir!* Not even a family as rich as the Grossfelds! All show and vanity! When we buried my father, God rest his soul, he wore his gold regimental ring, cuff links and studs, and the Glasshutter Uhrenfabrik gold watch and chain which my grandparents gave him on his wedding day. Six feet underground, God give him peace, he *still* wears them and always will. *Those* are the values *I* was taught to live by, not this business of snatching pearl chokers just before the casket is closed."

With this, he rushed out to resume work on his gravestones. Two minutes later the almost rhythmic sound of Herr Blober's hammer and chisel began to ring out through the quiet afternoon air, adding to the sound of Frau Blobel's heavy breathing as she struggled with the lining of Count Firsky's casket, of Gunther and me as we polished the casket, and the first inevitable buzz of blowflies attracted by the odor of Count Firsky's blood, and gathering en masse to pay it the most sacred homage of all, which is consumption.

A few moments later, Herr Brinkerhoff came by to examine the casket's seal, which he pronounced in perfect condition. "Myself," he said, nodding wisely to Herr Blobel, "I'd guarantee it for a century."

While Frau Blobel, her mouth full of safety pins, worked on the unitary all-purpose uniform which had been selected for the count, Herr Blobel pumped and thumped at what remained of the old man's body to make certain it contained as few surprise eructations as possible. I decided I had seen the main show and told Gunther I was going home.

"Wait a few minutes," he whispered, gesturing toward his father, "or you'll miss the best part of all."

Who could have resisted such an opportunity? I remained transfixed as Herr Blobel took a two-inch needle, threaded it with stout white silk, and went to work on the count's remarkably long foreskin, sewing it together drawstring fashion as tightly as a bag of gold dust. He then selected from a jar filled with some sort of preservative a piece of corklike material the size of a Ping-Pong ball. With a single jab of his needle he impaled it, drew the thread through it, squintingly estimated the distance between ball and foreskin and then, his sights clear, passed the needle through the ball at least two dozen times, secured it with a complicated knot, nipped the thread with his front teeth, dipped the ball in a white cream, and then, with infinite care, began to slip it into Firsky's somewhat shriveled anus, twisting it slowly until it sank into the position he desired.

The less one saw of the ball the less one also saw of the penis until finally neither was visible, which was precisely the effect Herr Blobel desired. Closure of other orifices was a much simpler process, after which hair-curling, shaving, dyeing, skin-taping, painting, rouging, wax-moulding, wrinkle-restoration, cheek-puffing, new eyelashes, and moustache-shaping completed the task of preparing him for eternal rest. By the time Herr Blobel had finished, Count Firsky even *looked* comfortable.

When it became known that the count had outlived three generations of Firskys, with the melancholy exception of the feeble-minded nephew; that the only surviving member of his regiment was ninety-six and confined to a home for the worthy indigent near Erlangen; that he had no close living in-laws; that his reclusive life had resulted in only two or three persons, aside from his valet, his gardener, and his doctor, who could even be called acquaintances; and that, contrary to popular belief, his estate was sound, of respectable proportions, and in excellent condition thanks to his lifelong hobby of accumulating debts, aging them for a decade or so, and then redeeming them at handsome discounts, all talk about the personal sacrifice of time and energy involved in trying to balance out the dead man's obligations and assets became transformed overnight into a community-wide eagerness to assist in every possible way with the sad task of winding up the deceased's affairs and assuring him a decent burial. In the end, however, the aggressive persistence of Herr Blobel, fortified by dark sacerdotal murmurs from Monsignor Schenkel of St. Boniface, routed the Samaritans and gave the monsignor and the undertaker control not only of the count's corpse but of his estate as well.

On the day of the funeral the sun rose so angrily that all four horizons quivered against the assault. The air grew acrid with prophecies and the earth turned unnaturally silent, as if that small funeral procession had consequences that one day would have to be reckoned with. Although it seemed impossible to believe that anything—anything at all—had been lost to the world with one old man's death, still and all the living were one less and the dead were one more, and no matter how insignificant the gain or loss, there *had* been change.

The local commandant of the Royal Grenadiers turned out an honor guard of fifty men plus six beplumed officers as honorary pallbearers. My father provided the drummer—his finest—to lead the cortege, feeling that the beat of a single drum would add much more solemnity to the occasion than the only band he could muster from Forchheim's limited supply of competent musicians.

In order to lend the event a sense of genuine community participation, the children of the Blessed Servants of Saint Veronica paid the penalty for their elders' lack of Christ-like charity. On one of the hottest days in local history the children of Forchheim were stuffed into their Saint Veronica uniforms, each handed a bouquet of withered and sometimes dehydrated field flowers, and compelled to follow the hearse, chanting hymns or prayers at Father Grimalden's (he was head man of the Blessed Servants) command. Behind the children straggled a disappointing handful of townspeople, the men fiery-faced from the heat and dripping sweat; the women wearing veils, which from time to time they surreptitiously used as fans.

Half a dozen dogs, amorously unbalanced by the wandering presence of a bitch in heat, brought up the rear of a procession dedicated to death with a carnival of lust, which ultimately could not fail to add more to the world's reservoir of life than was being withdrawn from it to the solemn beat of a drum, the slow clatter of horses' hooves, the rumble of hearse wheels over cobblestones, the shuffle of feet, and the occasional frantic warning of a Blessed Servant of Saint Veronica that it had to go to the toilet right now, couldn't wait another minute, and was as good as on its way already.

As we reached the open grave, Monsignor Schenkel, who had led the procession waving his censer as a baton to preserve the rhythm of his prayers and incantations, halted and faced the grave and the hearse which was backed up to its other end.

Gunther and I, who had marched immediately behind Monsignor Schenkel in the procession, now assumed positions at his left, it being our function to display the count's rather pitiable honors and decorations on small, gilt-fringed, black velvet pillows. Gunther's pillow displayed the Guard's Badge of the House of Wittelsbach; mine, his Meritorious Conduct Medal Second Class, which he was said to have earned by not running away from the Prussians during the Battle of Sadowa.

As the hearse doors creaked open to expose the splendor within, a mare of the hearse detail spread her legs and urinated resoundingly, while the Grenadier pallbearers, scrambling with as much dignity as possible to avoid the flood, slid the coffin onto its carrier, rolled it out of the hearse, and suspended it above the open grave with canvas straps.

It was at this precise moment that Gunther and I heard a sound which caused him to whisper in my ear, "What do they mean, 'sealed for fifty years'? I could have *soldered* this one together." I nodded, but there was nothing I could think of to say.*

---

* I began to write these notes, or whatever they may be called, in the hope that memory, such official records and documents as remained, and those portions of my diary that had not been lost or destroyed, if published now or in some future time, or, for that matter, ever, would add in some small way to the truth of my life, of my time, and of the world as I experienced it. Not selective truth, which is false by its very nature, but *all* of the truth, even that which is most loathsome.

Before sending the first two hundred pages off for the publisher's ap-

What we had heard, dimly to be sure, but nonetheless plainly, was a muffled wail of despair, a cry for mercy so anguished, so inconsolable, so desolate that I hear it still. Somewhere inside that casket, searching with sensitive paws for some small opening in her prison walls, sniffing at every seam in the casket's structure, burrowing frantically through Count Firsky's sixteen-percent-pure eiderdown pillows for a hole to crawl through or a puff of air to breathe, was Frija, lost and suffocating in the darkness.

---

proval I went through them with great care to check for conscious (as apart from accidental) violations of the standard I had set for myself. I found and corrected three small but self-serving errors and one forthright lie of which I was shamefully conscious even when I wrote it.

It was not Gunther alone who slipped Frija and her kittens into Count Firsky's coffin: It was Gunther and I together.—L.G.

♦ 6 ♦

Not all her tears can save Inge from becoming my toy, my bride, my slave

Whether it is a mercy or a curse I do not know, but youth by its very nature is callous, and the memory of youth is short. My shooting of the squirrel, the cruel yet somehow bewitching murder of my lovely doe with her seal-brown ears, my night visions of Frija trapped with her kittens deep under the earth in eternal search of an escape she will never find—the immediacy of these horrors passed quickly, although their mystery remains with me to this day.

I think there is a reason for this—a reason without which we would all go mad. I think that when the evils we have committed become too painful to remember we begin, stealthily and quite unconsciously, to eliminate them from the category of acts remembered, and find for them a place in the quite different category of acts we merely know about. Caesar died and Christ was born and Charlemagne was anointed Emperor of the West at Aix-la-Chapelle, but we do not remember them at all, we only know about them. Their reality we do not doubt, just as we do not doubt the reality of what we remember, but by shifting them from things remembered to things known we have put sufficient distance between them and ourselves to make life tolerable and civilization possible.

I doubt that this process is found only among the young. I remember the second and third epidemics of "war criminal" trials

(Germans prosecuting Germans for the "crime" of obeying wartime orders to execute a few thousand Jews!), which began in Hamburg in 1961; and I could tell by the surprise or astonishment or perplexity on the faces of the "defendants"—most of whom were known to me and several of whom were friends—that already it was becoming truly difficult for them to remember, in the sense that I use the word *remember*, the acts or crimes which they were charged with having perpetrated a quarter of a century earlier.

Already the healing process of shifting their "crimes" from events remembered to events simply known about was on its way to completion, having enabled them to build new lives, develop new careers, sire new families—in short, to become useful, valued, and sometimes distinguished members of the new German Reich, which war and the Allied surrender to Stalin had left behind as an infection in the heart of Europe.

These, however, are afterthoughts which belong elsewhere in this chronicle if I live long enough to deal with them in their proper order. In the meanwhile, the process of growing up in Forchheim continued as slowly as it always seems in the eyes of youth. Suns rose and set, weeks multiplied and then divided into months and months sedately turned to years. I became thirteen. Although I had no way of knowing it, the season for taking my pleasure of Inge lay at hand.

During the summers, at least three or four of the Kulig girls slept on the rear porch of their house to take advantage of the night's coolness, not to mention escaping from overcrowded bedrooms where in wintertime they must have lain three and four to each featherbed. I too slept on the porch of my father's house, our porch no more than fifteen paces from theirs, both porches canvased for protection against summer storms and for privacy as well.

The Kulig residence, like most of the better houses in Forchheim, contained an indoor water closet. One may imagine that in a family consisting of two adults and so many young and flighty girls, those demands of nature which recognize no rules of time or precedence sometimes outran the capacity of that one small utilitarian chamber to relieve them, particularly if two or three feminine necessities should coincide. This, of course, is merely an informed guess deduced from the fact that occasionally at night little Inge—who was eleven when I discovered her secret—found it sometimes convenient to steal from her porch into the garden and there, squatting primly, lift her nightgown and bedew the midnight grass with diamonds.

It is not remarkable that I, a healthy, lynx-eared boy, throbbing to the promise of this thirteenth year, lying on a cot no more than five meters distant from that porchful of sleeping Kulig girls, should ultimately hear the dainty hiss of Inge's salute and draw back my canvas to learn its source. Once discovered, I became a lad obsessed. Night after night I crouched on my cot in the starlight, crouched through the rising and waning of moons, crouched through the flash of summer storms and blazing showers of equinoctial meteors, utterly incapable of sleep or even sanity until Inge, in the remarkably various hours of her need, made use of her father's garden and returned to her bed.

In the beginning I observed those tender rites with no more than a voyeur's earnest curiosity. With the passage of time, however, curiosity changed to desire, and desire to inflamed resolution. Although as I have mentioned I was then but thirteen, already in my heart's mirror loomed the image of a bravo who strode through his dreams as the stuprator of all Franconia.

Hence, on a night never to be forgotten, in a moment of breathless purity and aching desire, precisely when the nightgown arose and the small haunch swung low to the summer lawn, Inge discovered a pilgrim at her shrine.

She started up at my first word, but before she could turn to flee, even before she could raise an alarm, my hand struck her wrist and held it fast while I pled my cause in desperate sibilants. There is an urgency about whispered speech in moments of stress which not only savors of conspiracy but invites—nay, almost compels—response in kind. Instead of rejecting my advance in tones that would alert her sisters on the porch, Inge compromised herself at the very outset by whispering back to me. In that instant she unwittingly became the partner of my conspiracy rather than its object.

I begged her to carry through the action I had interrupted. She refused. I persisted. She turned chill and haughty. I redoubled my pleas. She began to search her mind for answers more persuasive than simple negatives: It was not nice, she had not been going to do it anyhow, someone might see, her sisters would miss her, the dog might bark. Almost imperceptibly she had passed from flat assertions of her right to refuse into areas that verged upon my right to demand, thereby raising the issue to the level of debate in which each point for rejection implied the logical existence and even the possibility of a better one for acquiescence. Instead of discussing her right to dispose of her person as she wished, we now wrangled over my right to do with it as I desired. The mere thought of victory excited me almost to the point of suffocation. My temples throbbed, my throat tightened, my vision blurred. I threw logic to the winds. I gave myself over completely to hope and lust and awful humiliations. I gasped, I panted, I whimpered, I sobbed. I fawned, I groveled in the earth at her feet like a penitent pup. I begged. And then, in the midst of these wild entreaties, she yielded. Solemnly and almost reverently, she yielded.

I sank on my haunches to observe at close quarters a ritual that would change the whole course of my life. Shyly the nightgown drifted upward, sweetly the buttocks descended to enfold her young girl's form in the gracious posture of nature's most innocent act. Then, her face intent and grave, her eyes instinct with somber expectation, Inge sent forth her bright greetings to the night.

As the moment passed, but before she rose, I begged her to let me touch her skin. Just once, only once and no more, just once and then never again. Never. She whispered a sharp "No!" dropped her gown, and soared to her feet like a candle. But I was not to be denied. It seemed monstrous and altogether incredible that having surrendered one small part she could now withhold the rest. Stumping behind her on my knees like Quasimodo, wildly clutching the hem of her nightgown, I followed, whispered, prayed, and hung fast.

She paused, perhaps to save her gown from tearing, perhaps out of pity for me, perhaps from her own secret desire to reveal herself and be touched. For a long moment she stood perfectly still, as if thinking. I held my breath in respect. Slowly she turned her questioning face to mine. Her eyes explored me from naked feet and grass-stained knees to yearning upturned face. She turned away again, although not so far that she couldn't watch me from the corners of her eyes. Her arms sank to her sides. Her hands fluttered for a moment like butterflies against her flanks. Then, shyly and ever so delicately, her fingers plucked the folds of her gown to draw it upward. It rose like a ballet curtain, slowly, so slowly, ankles to slim calves to the swell of her thighs to the slender stem of her waist, stem of a lily in bud to the diaphragm's first curve, rising at last to proud shoulders encaped in billowing white.

I can see them still, those soft twin ovals gleaming like melons in the frost of moonlight, the left one made lovelier still by three delicate, wine-colored birthmarks. My palms caressed both halves gently, reverently, impartially, one stroke for each, or two, I can't remember, my fainting heart allowed no count. And then, with the most exquisite grace, everything blurred, withdrew, receded from my touch, dissolved. The curtain fell in snowy cascade to her feet. She fled across the grass and disappeared.

Thereafter no summer night found me absent from Herr Kulig's garden. I prowled those enchanted premises like a regnant tomcat. Sometimes Inge came to me, and sometimes she did not. Some nights she yielded while others found her coy, negative, maddeningly perverse. Then came a night when she appeared clad in nightgown, bathrobe, and slippers, her whole personality stiff with righteousness. She was not going to meet me again. I was nasty. All I wanted to do was watch her make water and look at her nakedness and touch her where nice people never touched. She was not going to meet me again in the garden or anywhere else. She had been wrong not to cry out when I first spied on her. Now she was through with it altogether. I was not to touch her, she had only come out to tell me.

She listened to my shocked objections with disdain, head shaking firmly, eyes bright with malice, mockery dancing in each curve of those smiling lips. Even worse, she kept a wary distance between us, sidestepping or retreating as I advanced, so that I hadn't even the chance to seize her wrist. I realized with something close to panic that she meant every word she spoke. Our enchantment had been shattered as abruptly as it had begun. Persuasion failing, I lunged for her, missed, and turned to blackmail.

"All right," I said, "then I'll tell."

"Tell what?"

"How you come out here in the garden at night. What you do."

"Nobody'll believe you. I'll say it isn't true."

"I'll tell how you let me look at you and touch you. I'll tell your sisters. I'll tell your father."

"I'll just say you're lying."

"I'll tell about your birthmarks. They'll know I'm not lying then."

She caught her breath for a moment. The triumph in her eyes turned cloudy at the first approach of fear, but she still clung to her position.

"You could have heard my sisters talking on the sleeping porch. Sometimes they make jokes about my birthmarks. Nobody would believe you."

"I'll tell how the birthmarks feel different than the rest of your skin. How they're rougher than the rest. How they're almost like little swellings. The only way I'd know that's by feeling them."

Gone now the mockery, gone the malice, gone the arrogance— all the proud certainties of resolution brought down in crashing ruins. Fear stood forth in every line of her face.

"You wouldn't do it!"

"I will too. I'll tell everybody."

"That isn't fair!"

"I'll not just tell them how the birthmarks feel, I'll tell them where you let me put my fingers and where sometimes I make you kiss me and where . . ."

I didn't trouble to finish the sentence, for already my palm lay softly where it willed.

From that time forward Inge was altogether mine. We met each night in Herr Kulig's garden, and in the daytime I took her to hidden nooks, forgotten attic corners, secret caves where I slipped off her clothes and held her in my arms and fondled her to our hearts' exhaustion. Face to face we surrendered ourselves to embraces passionately felt but only dimly comprehended. She was as various in her moods as a harem, sometimes ardent, sometimes filled with purling laughter, sometimes frightened and tearful, begging me to let her go. I would not do it. I could not do it. Her tears had no effect on me. When you have discovered and captured a mystery, a new world, an entirely different mode of existence, when you have made it your own and become its lord and master, tears are a wine to get drunk on.

♦ 7 ♦

For love of Gunther Blobel I am
cast like Lucifer from Paradise

I knew this happy state of affairs could not last forever. Summer
would end, the Kulig girls would move inside for warmth, and my
nocturnal observation post would become useless. There was, of
course, the extremely remote possibility of encountering Inge in
circumstances favorable to my purposes, but the possibility was so
remote as to border on the ridiculous. The truth is, I had so often
studied the construction of six pairs of long-armed, long-legged
Kulig-girl winter underwear, which seven months out of twelve
each Monday festooned their backyard clothesline, that I'm sure I
knew the odds far better than Herr Kulig himself.

The arms reached to the wrist, and the bodice braided itself
around the top of the collar bone. No provision at all was made
for the future or even immediate accommodation of budding
breasts. A small, button-up window at the rear was so precisely
measured to its purpose that a flat hand could scarcely have been
inserted between the soft flesh of her buttocks and the remarkably
small seat of her drawers without causing the fabric to rip at one
point or another.

There was, of course, another way, which might be called the
frontal attack, but the disadvantages here were at least as great as
with the other. The buttons at the front of her underwear began
at the sternum and marched in a straight line like soldiers down to

a point barely three inches above the navel. To proceed farther, even with a certain amount of cooperation, required the persistence of a monomaniac and the skill of a first-rate contortionist. This meant that from mid-October until late March all of Inge's wilder charms remained encapsulated in a winter chrysalis quite impossible to breach.

The end of our idyl, however, was accomplished by events fundamentally much more esoteric than woolen underwear or the winter's chill. It ended because of my friend Gunther Blobel, who was to become my closest comrade-in-arms during the war, my oldest friend and—despite the tragic contradictions of his death—my dearest.

It was characteristic of Gunther that although every girl in Forchheim fell in love with him at one time or another, he himself remained totally unaware of their attraction to him. Indeed, it was my desire to make him understand the mysteries which surround every female that caused my final rift with Inge.

When boys of the age we then were truly complement each other, when each learns freely to share with his chum every trait or quirk or quality of personality which the other lacks in his own, there grows between them a bond, an affinity, a union almost mystical, an affair of the blood which draws them closer to each other in the relationship of boy and boy than is possible in that other relationship between boy and girl, which is more in the nature of a game anyhow.

The reason is not hard to find. Boys, youths, even men, are invariably more comfortable with each other than they can ever hope to be with members of the more charming sex. Each makes fewer demands upon the other, and the emotional feeling between them is more profound because the tensions of sexual differences do not intervene to trouble their relationship. Their interests being the same, their functions, their desires, their dreams, and their goals provoke not the deceits of jealous rivalry, but the open honesty of friendly, manly competition.

Because of this they can impose, each upon the other, a relationship based upon perfect faith, which is altogether impossible to achieve in the context of male-female demands and gratifications. There is a heartiness, a manliness, a roughness of speech and gesture which conceals even from God's relatively perceptive eye the true nature of such comradeship, its depth, its constancy, its delicacy, its generous brooding urgency to share.

That, of course, was my dilemma vis-à-vis Gunther Blobel, my closest chum, and Inge Kulig, my little prisoner of love. I knew from endless hours of mutually shared speculations and declared intentions concerning the other sex that Gunther had never seen a girl as I had seen Inge, much less possessed or touched or been touched by one. Thus, even though I knew the vastness of his curiosity and the poignancy of his yearning, still I had told him nothing about the one thing he yearned for most. I had locked Inge up in my mind as a secret to be known only by me, I had hoarded her away from Gunther as a glutton hoards food while others starve. And yet . . .

The secrets of the human heart are unfathomable, as every crazed and cliché-ridden philosopher has taken pains to repeat, and as I, too, was shortly to learn. If one possesses an object whose enchantments are beautiful beyond the power of words to describe, does one hide it in a cellar, seal it off in a vault, lock it away in the secret darkness of one's most private room? Is it not the obligation of him who possesses beauty to show it? Is not the true purpose of beauty to be seen?—its only purpose?

I do not know. The old certainties have passed, and the new ones have changed from answers to questions. Perhaps those who bombed the Hofkirche of Chiaveri in Dresden are prepared to give us a lecture on the uses to which beauty should be put. The Bruehl Terrace, the Zwinger, the Georgenschloss in all its loveliness, its frescoed walls and vaulted ceilings—what are they now but rubble? Rubble and dust. Walk through that rubble, bestir that dust ever so gently and if the light is right you will see, here and there, a fleck of color no larger than the point of your pencil. Respect it, for it is something more than a micron of accidentally tinted dust, it is pigment from the brush of Carracci or Reni, of Rembrandt or Poussin. Nothing is left of all the beauty they created but this.

The English *always* knew what to do with beauty, didn't they? If you can't seize it openly, steal it. If you can't transport it whole, pack it off bit by bit. If there is no way at all to make off with it, then destroy it. Among simpler, less civilized folk there is found, almost without exception—and this has always been a matter of great perplexity to the British—a genuinely human desire to *share* it.

In any event, the decision I made was my own and I must live with it. My mother packed a picnic lunch, which I had correctly told her was for Gunther, Inge, and me. We walked into the summer woods and sat beside a small stream and ate our fill. Then we rested. I can see us there now as clearly as I saw us then over sixty-five years ago. Gunther lay full length on the ground at my left, his hands clasped behind his head, lifting it slightly so that his brooding, sun-smitten eyes could watch Inge, who sat on the ground at my right, her back propped against the log on which I sat between them. Eyes narrowed against the sun, she was counting with her forefinger the number of butterflies that had taken refuge from the afternoon heat beneath the leaves of a wild elderberry bush.

". . . eleven . . . twelve . . . thirteen . . ."

As I watched her sprawled so innocently beside me, her attention so completely absorbed in numbering butterflies, her young girl's body so indecently suffocated beneath untold layers of cotton swathing (I counted them in my mind because I knew what each of them was and the purpose it served), I could not—indeed I didn't even try to—prevent my mind from turning to thoughts of my power over her, and from there to the proof of that power through the testing of it, and from there to the actual use of a power that has already been tested and proved—the sheer excitement of using it any way I wished, from the gentle caress of a palm on her cheek to the unexpected cruelties of shame and undeserved humiliations.

I think the key word here is "unexpected" rather than "undeserved." Undeserved punishment is so common that almost everyone suffers from it in one way or another almost every day of his life. But *unexpected* punishment or humiliation is so rare—or so it seems to me, at least—that it falls into a special category of injustice and cruelty. Knowing this, feeling it in my heart to be true, nonetheless as we lazed there in the summer sun—three friends who had no reason to hurt each other—the special delight of testing my power over Inge by unexpectedly inflicting upon her the greatest humiliation I could imagine took form in my mind, at first no more than an abstract idea, a vagrant thought which insidiously turned to desire and then surprised even me by ending in passionate resolution.

Watching Inge there, still counting butterflies, soaking up life from the earth and the air and the sun, as careless of the moment as any other creature of the forest, secure from hurt or harm, I thought: "Lying there without a thought in your mind, and certainly without the slightest sense of fear, you haven't the faintest idea of what's going to happen to you in a few minutes, have you? Or what you're going to do because I tell you to do it? You may cry a little at first, but you'll get used to it. In two minutes, maybe three, it will begin to happen. In five minutes it will already *be* happening. Against your will. Without your consent. Without warning of any kind. Once begun, it will happen so very slowly that the pleasure of each second's revelation will linger on into the next. And the next, and the next, and the next, and the next. One by one your petals will drop to the ground until there is nothing left to touch your skin but summer air and my wandering hand. Here in the sunlight, stripped of everything but modesty and perhaps a few tears, you will perform the ultimate act of submission, so beautiful, so lovely, so bewildered, so sad, so sweetly compliant. Yet right now, counting butterflies on a summer day, the idea of doing what so surely you are going to do would seem, even if I told you, as unreal as any other fantasy that begins with the end of things and ends with their beginnings."

". . . nineteen . . . twenty . . . twenty-one . . . twenty. . . ."

I looked at Gunther, his eyes dreaming on her, and I thought, "You don't know what's going to happen either. Can you imagine her standing here before you without anything on, shy and naked and obedient and so close you have only to lift your hand to touch her skin? You can't imagine it, can you? Of course not. I'm the only one who can imagine it because I'm the only one who can make her do it."

I said, "Gunther."

His dreaming eyes turned from Inge to me.

"Yah?"

I said, "Would you like to see Inge without any clothes on?"

Inge stopped on twenty-eight. Her body tensed, but my right hand already encircled her wrist. Gunther's eyes, suddenly grown wide with bewilderment, turned from me to Inge and then back to me again. All he could say was "What?"

I said, "Because if you want to look at her, I'll let you."

"No!"

Inge was already on her feet, struggling like a cat to free her arm from my grasp.

"Let me go! I won't let him look at me! I won't let him see me!"

Her struggle and the urgency of her pleas told Gunther more clearly than I could possibly have explained in words that the favor I offered him was not the product of fantasy or even of sudden impulse; that it was at the least a practical possibility and at the best a likelihood.

I said, "Well, do you want to see her or don't you?"

He tried to say yes but his voice failed him. He could only nod and stare wildly at both of us and nod again.

Inge said, "Let me go!" and I said, "Not till you take your clothes off!" and she said, "I won't do it!" and I said, "Then I'll take them off for you!" and she said, "I won't let you!" and I said, "Then I'll give you a spanking!" and she said, "You wouldn't dare!"

She was eleven, I was thirteen; she was a girl, I was a boy. It was nothing to toss her belly-down across my knees and then, even though her legs kicked back at me furiously, to thrust her skirts upward, pull her underwear down, and vigorously spank what up to then I had only caressed. She began to cry and say "Ouch!" and "You're hurting me!" and "Please don't!"

Gunther was on his feet and beside me by now. Although his eyes were wild with desire, he said something that told me in a flash he would never do well with women.

"Don't hurt her," he said.

"I'm not hurting her, I'm only spanking her to teach her a lesson."

Then came Inge's voice, choked now, edged with panic.

"Ludwig—please don't spank me any more, *please* don't!"

I stopped. Her use of the word "spank" for the first time in conjunction with my name demonstrated her recognition of a fact which hitherto she had been unwilling to admit. All I could see of her was the back of her head and what remained visible of crossed arms that pillowed her brow against the log's rough bark.

"Will you be good?"

The back of her head bobbed up and down: "Yes."

"Will you do what I tell you?"

"Yes."

"All right, just a minute."

While Gunther stared down, eager as one fledgling vulture for the other's prey, I began to take her underpants off.

"You see," I explained, as an experienced man must to a tyro, "her underpants are already half off so we may as well take them all the way off."

He nodded eagerly. I slipped the underpants over the curve of her calves to her ankles. Inge remained perfectly still, perfectly silent, limber as a fresh-caught fish.

"Her garter-belt and stockings can wait till I take off her dress and her petticoats and her underwaist."

Gunther nodded again. I stretched her underpants over the bulge of her shoes, drew them free, tossed them onto the log beside me, and turned to her head at the other extremity of that limp body.

"You can get up now."

She rose to her elbows, snuffling a little, rolled off my lap, and came to her feet. As she reached her full height I took the precaution of encircling her wrist again. She stood for a moment, her eyes on the ground. Her free hand, doubled into a fist, ground the remainder of tears from them. I released her other hand, which descended immediately to smooth the disarray of her skirt. She knew I could outrun her, and on this day of days most certainly would. Also it gave me more pleasure to see her standing free, for if she did what I wished her to do without compulsion, the act of submission I hoped for would surrender not only her body into my keeping but her spirit as well. When her skirt was smoothed she lifted her face to us, fixed her eyes on Gunther for a moment, then turned to me.

"Don't make me take my clothes off," she said, "*please* don't."

"Why not?"

"Because it isn't fair."

"*What* isn't fair?"

"For Gunther to see me again. He already saw when you spanked me."

"Yes, but he didn't see everything."

"I don't want him to see everything! It isn't nice! *Please* don't make me!"

"Why not?"

"Because I'll be ashamed."

"You do it for me," I said. "You let me take everything off. You strip naked for me whenever I tell you to."

"Yes, but that's different."

"Why?"

Another long glance at Gunther, then back to me: "Because I *like* for *you* to see me."

"When you haven't got anything on? When you're naked?"

She nodded.

"Why?"

"Because I like you." She paused briefly. "And I like the way you look at me, too."

The guile of woman, the infinite guile which for five thousand years has transformed her weakness into strength and sent her spinning eons ahead of us in the long race for survival!

"You like Gunther too, don't you?"

"I *like* him but not enough to let him see me without my clothes on."

Is it any wonder that my heart melted? Is it any wonder that I said, "All right, you don't have to take everything off, just hold your skirts up so he can see."

There was another pause. She looked once more at poor Gunther, and then again, most lingeringly this time, at me.

"You won't let him touch me, will you?"

Gunther shot me a look of such wild entreaty that for one staggering moment—for one small instant in passing time—I realized that my power over him was as great or greater than my power over her.

"No," I said, "I won't let him touch you."

Her eyebrows arched, and for a moment I felt that she had cocked her head to one side.

"Then tell him."

I could feel the blood pounding at my temples. She was casting a charm, weaving a spell, invoking a mystery so strange in its promise, so exciting in the infinite range of its possibilities that when I turned to address Gunther I had to gulp for breath before the words came.

"You can't touch her," I said. "You can look at her but you can't touch her."

His voice, when he found it, came forth as a croak of despair.

"Why *not?*"

I turned back to Inge. She remained perfectly still, perfectly straight, her eyes flaunting promises I had never before even dared to imagine.

"Because I got her first. Do you think a girl undresses for you just because you ask her to? Well, she doesn't. You have to make her do it. Whether she wants to or not. There isn't a girl in this world who won't find herself someday with some boy who'll make her take her clothes off and let him do everything with her he wants to." I turned to Inge. "Isn't that so?"

"Yes," she said.

"Then pull your dress up. Not all the way. Just to below your belly-button. He doesn't need to see the rest."

Inge said, "He didn't *promise* not to touch me. All he said was 'Why not?' "

What was she doing to me? Why did she deliberately raise this raging storm in my heart, this fury of desire, this wild impulse to seize her and strip her and throw her on the ground and fill her with excrement?

"He doesn't *have* to promise, he knows he can't touch you anywhere, not even your little toe, unless I let him! I'll touch you so he can see all the places, but *he* won't touch you at all. Now pull your skirts up!"

Her voice, when it came, sounded far away and forlorn: "Why do I have to let him look at me when I don't want him to?"

"Because he's my friend and he's never seen what a girl really looks like!"

"Why does the girl always have to do it?"

"Do what?"

"Let people look at her when she's undressed?"

"Because a girl's different. You know that. She's different between her legs and when a boy wants to see her, she has to let him. Every woman too. *You* know that. Don't you think your father makes your mother take her clothes off whenever he wants to see her naked?"

"No! I don't believe it at all!"

"All right!" I said. "I was trying to be fair. If you'd pulled up your skirts like I told you to it would be all over by now. But you didn't do it, so now you have to take everything off. Right down to your birthday suit."

She looked at me for a moment, her eyes suddenly brimming with tears. In something close to a wail she said, "Do I *really* have to?"

I could scarcely breathe. I would suffocate if it went on like this any longer. The shame in her eyes, their meekness, their look of begging, of sorrow, of despair: Do I have to? Of *course* you have to! But that isn't what my voice said when finally I found it. She had gone too far. She had driven us into other and wilder latitudes from which now there could be no retreat.

"Of *course* you have to. And when they're all off I'm going to let Gunther touch you."

"Anywhere he wants to?"

I looked at Gunther, who was staring at her as if she were somehow sacred, a true religious apparition. Then I turned back to Inge and nodded.

"Anywhere he wants to," I said. Then, to make sure she understood, "Especially where the hair's beginning to grow."

Inge turned fiery red, and Gunther, babbling like a ventriloquist's dummy, said "Hair? Hair?"

I nodded. "It's beginning to grow between her legs," I said. "It's like silk. It's the softest hair you ever felt."

Inge said nothing. She simply stared at me, shaking her head as if at a wonder hitherto undiscovered, unrecognized and not yet fully comprehended. She stood before us, silent and immobile as a statue. Her eyes pivoted for a calculating instant to Gunther, who twitched and trembled like an old man, returned for a moment to me, and then wandered back again to Gunther.

"He's going to make me undress," she said, "because he thinks you *want* to see me that way. If you could only tell him that you don't want him to make me undress or—or let you touch me the way he said—then I won't have to. Don't you see, Gunther? I won't have to at all."

For a long moment Gunther stared from Inge to me and then back again to Inge. He opened his mouth three times before the words he was fighting not to say found utterance.

"It's all right," he said. "I . . . I'd like to see you that way . . . anybody would . . . but I"—he shook his head—"not if it makes you . . . I mean"—his words gathered speed as he fought his way toward the end of an answer he was already hating himself for— "I mean if that's the way you want it, I don't want to look at you or touch you any way except . . . except the way you want me to. Except the way you are right now."

She turned triumphantly back to me. She really thought she'd won. "You see?" she said, "He doesn't even want to see me!"

"He wants to all right," I said, "he's just afraid to say so. Well, *I* want to and I'm *going* to. *Then* we'll see what Gunther looks at. Now take off your clothes or I'll do it for you!"

"I'll do it," she said.

She bent low to pull her skirt off over her head, her hands fluttering for its beruffled hem.

I didn't see the rock at her feet, nor the hand that grasped it, nor the arm that threw it. For me there was only an explosion, a burst of starlight, a slow fall, and silence. Then, through a haze of blood, I saw Inge flickering like a moth through the forest and Gunther beside me, semaphoring with her underwear and yelling insanely.

"You forgot your underpants! Come back! You haven't got any pants on!"

That, of course, was the end.

♦ 8 ♦

I visit Forchheim en route to Nuremberg and the shadow of Inge darkens my beer

Being the beneficiary of my crime rather than its executor, Gunther got off lightly: a flogging, a written apology to the Kuligs, and the temporary loss of certain privileges.

For me it was an altogether different story. I had never before realized how greatly parents detest the peculiar beauty which makes their daughters female, or how madly determined they are to keep it hidden. Herr Kulig called on my father. My mother called on Frau Kulig. Herr Kulig conferred with Herr Blobel. Herr Blobel conferred with my father. Frau Blobel paid her respects to Frau Kulig. I was made to apologize to Herr and Frau Blobel for involving their son in so nasty an enterprise, and promise never to do it again. I was forced to make an appearance in the Kulig parlor for personal apologies (sound of soft sneaking footsteps upstairs, rustling skirts, vindictive titters) first to Herr Kulig, and then, as she entered the parlor, dressed in black, sniffling gently and dabbing her eyes with a lace handkerchief, to pink-eyed Frau Kulig herself. My regrets were sternly but reluctantly acknowledged, after which Herr Kulig indulged himself in what seemed to me a rather too detailed description of the atrocities a second attempt against their daughter's virtue would bring down upon my head.

I confessed to Monsignor Schenkel, who denounced my indecencies with a passion I had rarely heard from his pulpit, and imposed on me, as penance, the task of cleaning the toilets of St.

Boniface thrice daily for the next six months. During this unwholesome period of my life I discovered that one can learn a great deal more than sanitation from such work if he keeps his eyes open and knows something about normal below-the-belt realities.

I was also obliged to confess separately to Father Grimalden, whose sponsorship of the Blessed Servants of Saint Veronica, which was only one of his many duties, placed the welfare of Inge's soul under his direct supervision. He was a tall, thin man in his early thirties with enormously bulging blue eyes and a prehensile right forefinger that dredged his nostrils almost to the second knuckle.

The more I confessed the wrongs I had perpetrated on Inge the more wrongs he wanted me to confess, explaining that Inge was, after all, a Blessed Servant of Saint Veronica, and hence represented to him a graver moral responsibility than most. Was it indeed true that I had forced her into this ghastly situation? I had spanked her? Where? Oh God forgive you, not on the poor child's bare skin? Had she cried? Had I truly threatened to undress her? Would I have done so but for the rock that rendered me unconscious? Was it true that I had undressed her or seen her undressed prior to the afternoon in question? Approximately how many times? When? Where? What did she say or do? What did she look like?

When I began to suspect that Father Grimalden was getting as much sheer animal joy out of the situation as I had, that he was in short enjoying for nothing pleasures for which I would be forced to endure the most brutal penance, I began to embroider my confession with attractive little lies which I hoped would not only add to his pleasure but also diminish in some degree whatever penance he might have it in mind to inflict on me.

The sort of sin to which I had just confessed, I told him, was not something peculiar only to the relationship between Inge and me, it was happening more often than either of us suspected, and to some of the prettiest girls in town at that. I could almost hear the increased rapidity of his breath through the thin black curtain that separated us. What girls? he asked. What were their names? Didn't they object? Didn't they think of going to their parents for help? Or to him, their priest, for guidance and moral strength? And the boys? What were *their* names? Didn't they realize they were endangering their immortal souls for a few moments of fleshly delight?

I agreed with everything he said, nodding my head so vigorously that by the end of my confession, which must have been one of the longest in the history of St. Boniface, my neck was actually sore. My penance, however, made the whole ordeal worthwhile: one hundred Hail Marys for one hundred days running, plus a promise that I would send to Father Grimalden for confession and moral salvation every girl I knew whose underpants were being misused or removed by acquaintances who perhaps did not understand the damnable consequences of the sins they were committing. I swore to do so in the name of the Father, the Son, and the Holy Ghost, received Father Grimalden's "blessings on you, son," and took my departure.

In addition to the social and religious penalties imposed on me, there were quite separate familial reactions. For three nights running my father took me out onto the back porch and flogged me soundly before thrusting me into my bed. I envisioned Inge's vengeful smile as she listened to those powerful blows and my occasional reactions to them. My allowance was suspended for three months, my household privileges for six. I was assigned to extra and always backbreaking tasks: I cut wood, I shoveled coal, I moved dirt, I cleaned chicken run, horse yard, and garbage dump. I stacked and moved and piled and heaped and carried away and brought back again. The whole while I could feel Inge's mocking eyes secretly following every step of my loathsome routine, celebrating her triumph, dreaming of further torments to come. Each morning, from the beginning of that long ordeal to its end, found me asking myself *was it worth it?* and each evening found me answering *yes*.

Looking back now at the guilt and innocence of that first and tenderest love affair, I perceive that although my behavior was completely adoring, it failed somewhat in gallantry. On the other hand, Inge suffered no harm, since at thirteen I was still incapable of carrying my project through to its logical conclusion. For all my intentions, she still remained *intactus*.

Beyond that, I am not at all convinced her eagerness to be rid of me was as deeply felt as she pretended. In the very nature of woman from cradle to coffin there exists a deep yearning, even a necessity, for male compulsion when the most intimate secrets of her being are to be disclosed. Innate modesty prevents her from drawing aside with her own hands a veil that is more appropriately rent by those of a man. She shrinks from the responsibility of giving at the very instant when she wishes most to give; her nature calls out to force, it yearns for an assault so fierce, so relentless, so savage, so utterly without pity or remorse that all her defenses collapse through sheer exhaustion. Thus the portal is forced and the palace ravaged without consent. Only then can she taste without guilt the sweets of surrender; only then can she sense the ravishing joy of the conquered in final conquest of her conqueror.

That the loss was clearly mine in Inge's case by no means meant the victory was hers. Others would pick up the bright banner which I had been compelled by youth and fate to abandon, and one of them, especially beloved of God, would harvest the fruits of a conquest I had merely begun. Twenty years and more were to pass before I saw with my own eyes how triumphantly she had survived the frenzies of a summer, which then she may have thought her time of trouble.

Our movement, after a decade of bitter struggle and savage losses, had stormed the summits of power and held them against all comers for three exhilarating years. The Red Front and its allies had been driven from the streets; the trade unions had been taught the lesson of patriotism and their properties nationalized; the Reichstag had been purified first of Communists, then of Social Democrats, and finally of Hugenberg; the Party itself had been cleansed and consolidated only weeks before by the purge of Roehm and his crew of homosexual adventurers, and only the eternal Jew remained. *"Oremus pro perfidis Judaeis."* But why? And particularly why on Good Friday?

The whole Party, in short, was caught up in one of those healthy periods of reorganization that always presage great enterprises to come, and I, as a result, found myself driving the autobahn from Munich to Nuremberg, having been temporarily detached from my unit for special duty at the headquarters of Julius Streicher, Gauleiter of Franconia, publisher of *Der Stuermer,* and chairman of the Central Committee for Defense against Jewish Horror and Boycott. The Gauleiter at that time was felt to be enforcing certain of the new racial measures (they had not yet been systematically codified as later they would be in the Decrees of Nuremberg) with too large an excess of enthusiasm over discretion. It is one thing to control and even sequester potential enemies of the state, but quite another to publish such vivid details of the action as openly to confirm what the Foreign Ministry has denied before the whole world as a typical example of international Jewish propaganda against the German state and people.

As I approached the outskirts of Erlangen, something in the quality of the older houses—their look of solid bourgeois comfort, their steeply timbered roofs, their flowering windowsills—filled me with memories of youth so poignant that when I reached a point in the business section where a sign still announces the turn-off leading through Forchheim to Bamberg, sheer nostalgia compelled me to take it. It was less than an hour's detour each way; I'd have time for a beer and still reach Nuremberg by sundown.

It was summer again, and market day in the town square. The

housewives of Forchheim moved through the sun in slow processional, passing from stall to shaded stall as their market bags swelled fatter and fatter—stuffed cornucopias in gentle sway against the solid flesh of peasant madonnas out of Breughel. As I sat there alone, dreaming into the pure topaz of a Loewenbrau shot through with shafts of gold and dappled pools of sunlight, a shadow fell across my table, abruptly changing the gold of the brew to brown. In that same moment, even before the shadow passed and the topaz flashed fire, the air turned redolent of woman and of little girls on hot summer afternoons.

I sat perfectly still, transfixed by the spreading glow in my blood, by the swift erections of papillae which traced the course of my spine, savoring a distillation of flesh and skin and thigh and loin so pungent, so sultry, so acid-sweet, so urgently demanding that no man who had ever known the spell of its languor could doubt its source or forget it.

I lifted my eyes as the shadow slid from table to cobblestones and slowly retreated toward the market stalls beyond. She wore a low-necked sleeveless cotton frock printed with arsenic leaves against a field of crimson roses. She had gathered her flaxen hair in a knot at the base of her neck, but not all of it. Wisps escaped everywhere. To eyes narrowed against the slanting sun they formed a nimbus, a glow announcing the beautification of contented flesh. The powerful spread of her buttocks sang hymns to the triumph of culinary art over a bounteously groaning pantry. They rose and fell against each other like handsome fresh-killed hams, setting up a tumult among the roses, which seemed to cluster in that place more thickly than anywhere else: they huddled together and then dispersed, they minced and bowed and swayed like a community of overrouged coquettes caught in the passing eye of a summer whirlwind.

The amplitude of her arms, although in perfect proportion to the trunk, prevented them from swinging straight and free as they had in springtime years. Their movement now was short, choppy, vaguely semaphoric. She was, in fine, both caricature and idealization of the classic German *Hausfrau*, serene and strong and solid, as content with her position as the mere fact of her existence contented others.

Thus she departed from me, rolling gently as a full-sailed brigantine through placid seas—departed without even knowing she had approached. The warmth of her scent still lingered above my beer as she thrust aside a dangling fringe of sausages and slaughtered hares and vanished into the cool shadows of a butcher's stall.

Inquiry established that little Inge, in prosperous union with her second cousin (a wholesaler of cabbages and other produce), had matched each of those charming birthmarks with a sturdy child. I like to think, and have no reason for believing myself wrong, that by now she recalls with pleasure those happy mysteries into which she was at least symbolically initiated by the music master's son so many years ago in Forchheim, when the world was young and the word "hope" could be uttered without a curse to qualify it.

◆ 9 ◆

*With the Wandervoegel in the last
golden summer of my youth*

Anno Domini 1913: the last year of the twentieth century in
which absolutely nothing happened: the Jews in the Reichstag
screwed up their nerves to the point of passing the first vote in
history against an Imperial Chancellor; some spies were found
operating in the Krupp works; there was trouble, but very little,
about the Zabern affair in Alsace-Lorraine; the First Balkan War
ended, and the Second began and ended also, but they were small
wars between petty peoples whose fates concerned no one; Germany led the world in steel production—fourteen million tons to
America's ten to England's six—but that did not make me nor
those I knew any happier than had the figures been reversed; the
Belgians introduced universal military service; the Reichstag
passed an act that doubled the amount of gold reserves for the
military; the King of Greece was murdered in Salonika (how
could I then have known the blood relationship with Salonika
that *I* should develop before I died?); Princess Victoria Luise of
Prussia married Prince Ernst August of Cumberland, Pretender to
the throne of Hanover, and the Tsar was there and so was the
King of England and, of course, the Kaiser, still grieving, they
said, in his loneliness for Prince Eulenburg; Ernst August
ascended to the throne of Brunswick, ending the regency of Johann Albrecht; crazy Otto was deposed in favor of Ludwig III,

who was rumored to be only half-crazy at the very worst. Anno Domini 1913. That and nothing more.

What an innocent year it was! Crisp ortolans and wild strawberries in clotted cream (or so I'm told), amongst which dolls and puppets and princes and kings of kingdoms half the size of postage stamps moved with such grace, such elegance, such splendor, and even such beauty (who could fail to drop a tear for Elizabeth of Austria?) that from the beginning of their lives to their very ends they were actually considered to possess a significance far larger than the tiny sum of the earth's atmosphere their living carcasses actually displaced.

I am reminded of it because the other day one of those nameless, joyless, old-stocking-odored creatures who call themselves Jehovah's Witnesses (Beata and I staffed our house at Auschwitz with them) knocked at my cottage door and harangued me for half an hour because the world was coming to so terrible an end so quickly that I'd scarcely have time to repent before the all-encompassing flames reduced me to ash and unforgiven sins. Without mention of my experience with human ash, I tried in vain to explain to her that the world ended in 1919 and that, unbeknown to her, we have been living the resurrection ever since, whether in heaven or hell or purgatory being entirely beside the point. She hadn't the faintest notion what I was talking about.

The truth is that although she was by no means young, neither was she old enough to have the remotest idea of what the world was like before it died. Only I, it seems, dream back to that magical summer of 1913 in what was destined to be the gentle climax of half a century of peace—the last of those mysteriously golden summers before the dream exploded like a festering corpse in the broiling suns of mid-July, and the most believing of all generations in the long history of Europe toasted each other with beakers of blood and pus and then, like surprised children, sank back in their millions to fill a continent with graves that ended the dream for all time.

When the dreamer dies, the dream dies with him and it dies forever. What it leaves behind is also forever. Don't look for change, don't look for anything better, look only at your own mirror image in every other human face and recognize the dreamless animal for which there is no comfort and from which there can be no escape. What began with man as god has ended with animal as man, and there's no way to change it now.

But O my God and all His Blessed Beings, how beautiful it was *then*—low fields, broad rivers, winding trails, deep woods, far-gleaming peaks, the earth, the sky, the yellowing sun, the moonlight, and all the young boys no longer boys but men. Gunther and I, having put Inge far behind us, were now fifteen. The mortician's son, by some miracle of growth and attenuation, had turned slim as an arrow and almost two inches taller than I, who was plainly destined to grow square and strong but never tall.

For two summers now (1913 being, of course, the last) Gunther and I had tramped the summer countryside as Wandervoegel, clad in leather shorts, stout boots, lederhosen, rucksacks, carrying a bedroll or blanket strapped to our backs, eating where we might, sleeping beneath the stars in fields and forests, by lakes and running rivers, drawing our strength from the earth and each other, eschewing all that came from the city or stank of age or blew from the West.

We were, in those opening years of the century, already in revolt against our bourgeois fathers, our bourgeois schoolmasters, our bourgeois government, yes, even our bourgeois Kaiser. Our revolt looked not toward the future but to the past, to the far deep Teutonic past when each worked for the other and all for the whole, when unquestioning obedience to a leader of our own bone and blood and spirit offered—as it still does—a far more joyous concept of freedom than the street pedlars' freedom to swindle each other through "elected majorities" in that corrupt and corrupting commercial network of parliaments and exchanges and shops and factories and unions which Western democracy has so carefully fashioned for the destruction of the Teutonic state and soul and peoples.

Matthew, Mark, Luke, and John, Esau and Job and Baal—these were not the holy or unholy names we called upon. When it wasn't Wotan or Siegfried who sang in our blood, it was the voice of the East, the voices of Nietzsche and Stefan George, of Langbehn and Lagarde, the voice of Hegel right side up, the philosophers of materialism, the voices of a blood brotherhood as different from Western Europe as Loki from Christ himself. Not against each other but for each other, for all, freely for all, freely obedient, held in total thrall by devotion to the leader. We had left the city, the merchant, the professor, the politician, the banker, the Jew, the self-proclaimed virgin and her fraudulent son who was killed at last by the Jews—we had left them forever behind as we searched for something older, simpler, and infinitely more pure: for something, in short, worth dying for.

When I say that Gunther and I were of the Wandervoegel, I mean both more and less than the word actually conveys. The Wandervoegel was composed of many groups, some under the leadership of teachers and others without formal organization or steadfast identity or aims. Some had sworn against the eating of meat, some were pledged to pacifism, to atheism, to celibacy, to epicureanism, to self-abnegation, to mortification of the flesh, to religious fanaticism; some called themselves the Brotherhood of the Soil, Pathfinders, Wanderers into the Void, Youth Culture, Seekers of the Message, the Folk Brotherhood, Penitents of the North, Voyagers to Nowhere, etc., etc. Many tramped the woods and fields as established groups, but others moved at random from group to group in what became known as the Journey to Nowhere—a term so dear to the heart of German youth that in the end it became its goal.

Nonetheless, as we drifted from Forchheim to Bamberg and beyond, a whole concatenation of secret messages began to spell out our destination: words scrawled on a rock, a note floating in the breeze, glances exchanged around the campfire, a general drift of movement down trails and across the banks of rivers, a feeling in the air, a whispering in the wind, a yearning, an urgency, a silent passion that raged from one end of Germany to the other until, at some point in the journey, all of us, in our thousands and tens of thousands, knew, without having consciously chosen, that we were going to Hoher Meissner and that no power on earth could now prevent us from arriving at our destination. It was as if the old Teutonic Gods had spoken to us.

Outside of Bamberg we slept beside the Regnitz for two nights before following its course to the river Main. There we fell in with two other comrades, Karl Rader and Paul Koch by name. They were close to our own ages, both from Nuremberg, and, to our surprise and perhaps also theirs, they too were going to Hoher Meissner.

On our first night together, after we had boiled and eaten our barley *Schleim* (fortified by a sausage the one named Karl had stolen from a butcher's stall and cut into quarters and added to it), we lay back on the ground while the one named Paul read from Stefan George by the glow of our cooking coals:

THE QUESTIONER: You whom I cut down from the gallows, will you speak to me?

THE HANGED MAN: When amid the curses and the shouts of the whole town I was dragged to the gates, I saw—in each man who threw a stone at me, who set his arms akimbo full of contempt, who with staring eyes pointed his finger at me across the shoulder of the man in front—I saw that one of my crimes was latent in each, only narrower or hemmed in by fear. When I came to the place of execution and the aldermen showed both disgust and pity for me in their stern faces, I was moved to laughter: "Do you not realize how greatly you need the poor sinner?" Virtue—against which I had offended—on their faces, and on the faces of decent wives and girls, however real it may be, can only glow as it does if I sin and I do! When they put my neck into the noose my malice showed me my future triumph: I the buried man will enter as a conqueror into your brains ... and I will be active in your seed as a hero about whom songs are sung, as a god ... and before you have had time to realize it I shall bend this stiff bar round into a wheel.

That is what we were thinking of in 1913; that is what we dreamed before our council fires; and that is what, as our lives translated themselves into action, dominated the world's history for more than half a century—and still does.

After leaving the Main we crossed north through Bad Kissingen and thence to the headwaters of the Fulda which would lead us to Kassel, south of which lay Hoher Meissner. There, beside our campfire on the river bank below Hersfeld, we were joined by a remarkable one-eyed comrade of seventeen, also bound for Hoher Meissner.

His name? "How can anyone say 'my name' when it isn't his, it's something chosen for him by others and attached to him without his permission? I have no name. None of us have a name, when you come to the truth of it; we've only got something for others to call us by. What I am called by I have chosen for myself. Call me Fenri, which is short for Fenrir, and if you don't like it then go to hell and I'll go to Hoher Meissner by myself."

Fenrir, chained by the gods, who, shattering the earth with his struggles, broke free, sailed south to the field of Vigrid, and there allied himself with the giants in that last terrible assault on Valhalla: "Fire spurted from his eyes and nostrils" wrote the Ancient One; "from his gaping jaws dripped blood; his upper jaw touched the heavens, his lower jaw brushed the earth."

So Fenri he was. We were very much for every man having his own taste, his own way, his own life—for having, in short, himself.

"Next you'll be wanting to know about my eye."

We shook our heads, but none of us could avoid stealing a

glance at the great, staring, milk-white curdle of phlegm which he'd had the courage to call an eye.

"It's no matter," he said, "I'm not ashamed of it. I was milking a stupid bitch of a cow in my father's barn and she swished her tail and caught me across the open eyeball with it. I rushed to the woodpile outside for an ax and came back at her. Good God, you've never heard such bawling. She backed and turned and shuffled and bellowed and spurted blood like the town fountain while I, with only one eye to see her through, hacked away at her eyes and nose and the skull between her horns and finally her neck until at last she sank to her knees and I slit her throat with my hunting knife.

"By the time my father got there I had her strung up by her heels and was bleeding her. He looked at the cow for a moment, then at me, then at my lost eye. 'You'd have done better to follow scripture and make it an eye for an eye,' he said. 'We'd still have the cow and her milk instead of her dead weight in summer meat, and you'd be no worse off than you are now.' I forsook him and his house and his farm and his name that very day, and I've never missed any of them since. I'm a Holsteiner, you know. We're good haters."

We agreed almost too fulsomely. There was something about the quality of his eyes that made agreement with him particularly easy. He regarded us for a moment with his one astonishingly good eye and then said, "Why pretend to understand something you don't? I am one of Nechayev's doomed men. By my own choice I have no personal interests, no affairs, no sentiments, not even a name of my own, as you know." He pawed through his rucksack, withdrew a tattered paperbound book, and menaced us with it like a weapon. "Bakunin and Nechayev," he said. "Men. More than men. Truth-tellers and destroyers. So long as we understand that's the way I unchangeably am, we'll have no trouble. Beyond that you'll find me a good man in a just fight and the meanest bastard that ever pulled knife in an unjust one."

So it was. Who wanted to argue with him? Thus it happened

that five of us left Kassel and moved from the bottomlands of the Fulda and Eder through the forest of beech and oak and sweet-smelling conifers which marks the first rise of the land as it approaches the breast of Hoher Meissner itself.

Late in the afternoon we paused beside a shallow stream to drink and bathe our faces. From somewhere above us on Hoher Meissner we could hear, though very faintly, strains of *The Song of the Freebooters* rising and falling on the summer breeze. Nearer at hand the wild hunting cries of barnswifts proclaimed that particular hour in which the late afternoon sun, casting shadows against the east, steals the disguise of ordinarily translucent flying insects and lays them hopelessly open to their enemies.

The swifts, in their terrible need, cry *food! food! food!* and the sun-dancing insects die so quickly after they're born that their lifetime's history can be encompassed within a few fleeting heartbeats between the void from which they came and the void to which they have returned as food for that soft-breasted, full-feathered flight of reptiles which spiraled that afternoon more wildly toward the apogee than I had ever seen them before, wheeling and circling, darting and diving and twisting, reversing, stalling, looping, stabbing the air with their terrible beaks, crying hunger against that later moment when the light fades, the slaughter ends, the swifts sink to their nests, and the insects conceive new generations for tomorrow's hunt.

Suddenly those faint cries from above which had absorbed our lazy attention gave way to a cacophony of shrieks much louder, much closer at hand. We leapt to our feet, scrambled through a growth of underbrush and briar, and emerged into a barnyard clearing.

A peasant's thatched hut stood at its far end, together with a woodshed, a smokehouse, three half-shaded pigsties, and, at the center of the complex, a wide-eaved two-and-a-half-storey barn. Alongside the barn a peasant stood on a massive wood plank supported at either end by half-filled rainbarrels swarming with larvae.

Sure-footed on his plank, the peasant slashed with his spade at perhaps ten generations of swallow nests, each the exquisitely beaded work of an architect with instinctive understanding that beauty is inseparable from strength.

A litter of fragmented day nests, feather-down linings, tiny white cinnamon-spotted eggs, gluey yellow yolks, limp, unborn cadavers, the naked newly hatched, and crushed fledglings covered the plank on which he stood and spilled over onto the ground beneath it.

The peasant was squat, big-boned and filthy, with the receding horny brow, high cheekbones, and slow-blinking, water-colored eyes that always betray the Slav. His children—a boy of ten and a girl somewhat younger—pale-faced, stunted, bare feet covered with blood and foul-smelling yolk, hands hot and sticky with bits of claw and beak and matted feather-down still clinging to them, looked even less human than their father. From each nostril of each blank-faced child a trail of yellow snot descended to the brink of each upper lip there to tremble a moment before being trapped by the flick of a tongue and quickly sucked inward from view.

Between huge gulps of snot they fought each other in shrieking competition "No, no!" "That one was *mine!*" "You killed *my* bird!" for the pleasure of smashing still unbroken eggs, crushing to death those that lay panting with the first suspirations of life, or wildly tracing the looping, erratic flights of bewildered fledglings that rarely rose more than half a meter before life was crushed from them by the hot, sticky paws of a playful child.

Suddenly Fenri's voice rang out, surprising us almost as greatly as the peasant: "Stop that, you Goddamned *scheisser Sauhund!*"

All sound but the lamentation of the swallows gave way to frozen silence as the peasant and his children turned to us and stared, each trying to comprehend the fact of our existence, the peasant himself obviously searching for some response to a circumstance that clearly could not have seemed stranger to him had we been talking bears, and Fenri the Kaiser himself leading the

Household Guards at full charge toward the foul anesthetic stench of those pigsties on the nearest side of the barn. The two children nervously increased their consumption of snot.

When at last the peasant found his voice he managed to croak: "What's it any business of yours?"

At this point Paul Koch intervened, almost, it seemed to me, in the voice of Stefan George: "Because birds don't belong to you or anybody else and nobody's got no right to kill 'em!"

"Then *you* take 'em, you little son of a bitch!" said the peasant. "They muck up the place, and this is my place, and I don't want it mucked up."

Gunther beside me pointed to the pigpens. "There's no muck from swallows that compares to your damned pigs," he said.

"You're bums and tramps and beggars," said the peasant. "You've none of you never done an honest day's work in your life. Get off my property before I take this spade to you instead of these damned shit-drippers."

He turned his back to us, lifted his spade, and knocked down a full three feet of nests. The swallows redoubled their protests; the children hopped with renewed delight from one murder to the next and the next and the next.

With something between a howl and a roar, Fenri leapt into the still-falling debris and kicked a barrel from beneath one end of the bird-killer's plank; the peasant pitched face forward into a jelly of dead birds and feathers salted with barnyard filth and guano and soaked with stale rain matter. The children once again froze, gaping with stupefied disbelief at the sight of their hideous father now so astonishingly brought low. Fenri hurled himself astride the peasant and began to tear at the rope that served as a belt for his trousers.

"Strip his ass and turn him over a barrel," he yelled. "Give him the same medicine he probably gives his snot-eating kids and his shit-eating wife if he's got one."

Suddenly all of us were on top of the peasant, stripping him of his boots, socks, trousers, his unbelievably filthy underdrawers. A woman rushed screaming from the hut at the end of the clearing, the pigs set up a deep-throated gabble, the peasant fought back with grunts and curses, and the children, staring imperturbably, sucked snot. By the time the woman joined us, her man, naked from the waist down, lay neatly pinioned over the barrel, held down by the four of us, while Fenri, using his own broad belt, applied good hot leather to his hindside. The peasant grunted with each slash, while the woman screamed, "Stop it! He's a good man! You have no right! He tries to keep the place clean, that's all—he just tries to keep the place clean!" and the children simply stared, utterly immobile save for the pistonlike flicker of their snot-sipping little tongues.

At the first streak of blood Fenri withheld his belt. "Turn the bastard loose," he said. In doing so, we flipped him off the barrel and onto the ground on his back.

One arm was folded over the upper half of his face. To the astonishment even of his dreadful children, he was sobbing bitterly.

"Heinrich," moaned his wife, "oh Heinrich, Heinrich . . . !"

Angrily, almost convulsively, the peasant turned himself over onto his belly. "Shut up!" he said. "Go away! Leave me alone!"

Fenri dropped quickly to his knees beside him, seized the back of his neck, and turned him once more belly-upward.

"Count those nests!" he said, not to the peasant but to all of us. "Count 'em on both ends and the other side too." "You count too," he said to the gaping children, and then, to their mother, "and you. Be sure you don't miss a one. We're going to the top of the Hoher Meissner and we'll be back in exactly three days, and if there's one nest missing"—he shook a forefinger directly between the peasant's eyes—"just one single missing nest, do you know what you're going to do? You're going to smack your lips and run your tongue around the edge of them to make sure you didn't miss a single little piece, and then you're going to dip your snout in for the next course. Do you understand?"

The peasant, whose eyes were still flooded with tears, gulped twice, found enough voice for a grunt, and nodded.

"Then *say* you understand. Say it!"

The peasant fought for breath. Then, in a voice that sounded astonishingly like a child's, he said, "I understand."

Fenri said, "Good." Then, followed by the rest of us, he started briskly across the barnyard toward our point of entry. The children still stood like statues, although the woman rushed forward and sank to her knees beside her sobbing husband. We could hear her voice crooning to him as we crossed the barnyard. Then, as we started into the undergrowth at its edge, a child's cry caused us to turn and look back.

Everything had changed. Now it was the woman who lay on the ground. Her peasant-master, half-naked but on his feet and howling imprecations, belabored her with a heavy stick. The children, weeping loudly and snotting more copiously than ever, vainly tried to stay his hand. Although I presume I should have felt sorry for them, it seemed to me that for the first time since we had broken into their lives they were dealing with a situation that every one of them had been born to understand.

♦ IO ♦

*"For their vine is the vine of Sodom,
and of the fields of Gomorrah: their
grapes are clusters of Gall; their
clusters are bitter"*

July 13, 1913: "Last night I had my way with Gunther Blobel."

Those are the first lines of a diary which I began on the morning of July 14, 1913, and have continued intermittently ever since.
I say "intermittently" because there were periods of several weeks
during which I neglected it entirely, while at other times it required fifteen or twenty pages to empty myself of the feelings
which gushed forth to fill its pages when I least expected or even
wanted them to.

The diary was my father's idea. "All men of any intellectual
substance realize that what seem the most trivial moments of
their lives often serve to introduce or explain or even foretell the
most important. Dates and hours and places and associates carry
such significance that records of them should be preserved as
carefully as one records the state of one's financial affairs, the degree of one's service to the state, or the regular functioning of
one's body. What an absurdity it is (and one that happens all the
time, incidentally!) that an ordinarily intelligent man should lose
a legal action or suffer the brunt of scandal because of a memo not
written or a diary note not made.

"A man must live his whole life on the assumption that no matter how close his friendships with other men may be, or even with those bound to him by the most sacred cords of consanguinity, there may and probably will come a time when he finds himself under oath in magistrate's court confronted by the false testimony of his former friend or present kinsman. If, in this supremely important moment, he is unable to produce a note or memorandum or even a diary notation—one perhaps recalled after the fact and jotted down in its proper place—he is very likely to lose his case.

"The oath to speak the truth in such matters has no practical value at all because it's our natural assumption that both sides are lying. The side which enters the courtroom without substantiating physical evidence of *some* kind is generally considered too foolish to be granted the presumption of innocence and probably too guilty to claim it. However, the litigant with a decent white collar, a set of well-filled diaries, and a case bulging with documents obviously knows what he's about and generally wins not only the case but public approbation as well.

"Therefore keep a diary wherever you go. No matter how trivial, write something in it every day including the Sabbath. Particularly on warm summer Sabbaths, because they have lately become notorious for criminal seduction and other offenses of like nature."

I opened my diary with an account of that remarkable night on Hoher Meissner because, although my father had given it to me on Christmas, and although I accepted his opinion of the importance of detail (as I respected most of his opinions), nothing had happened during the first half of 1913 that seemed important to record even as detail.

Indeed, it was not until much later, when in the midst of what promised to be an interminable sexual drought, that I realized my adventure with Inge in that town and at that time had been one of those rarities which are almost never appreciated or understood until tried a second time. Only then does one realize that such games are almost always lost, and must be handled with the utmost delicacy even when hope has surrendered to the infuriating knowledge that one's purpose would just as successfully be achieved by a swift slap across the cheek as by presentation of the Koh-i-noor itself in a platinum case.

Sexually, my life had been a blank since that fatal afternoon, which now seemed so many years ago, when I misjudged my powers over Inge and lost her altogether. Indeed, my whole relationship with Inge had resulted from the accidental coincidence of propinquity and good luck, which I daresay happened to no more than two or three members of my generation; for in Forchheim and its neighboring communities sex without wedlock carried with it the same connotation as leprosy, and the measures taken to stamp it out were almost as maniacal.

Aside from finding them with an extra pair of drawers of the wrong sort, as I was caught with Inge's (something not to be expected every day), the parents of adolescent boys had a much easier time of it than those of pubescent girls. Threats, lectures, deprivation of privileges, and an occasional thrashing were generally considered sufficient to discourage all but the most persistent symptoms of male amatory enterprise.

Beyond this, the fathers of Forchheim went no farther. Being males in a community entirely governed by red-nosed, fat-bellied, thick-necked, beer-swilling males with limp white collars, sweat-circled armpits and drooping crotches, the idea of masculine beauty itself, much less of any even moderately intelligent woman being tempted by it, never entered their minds. They believed that women are drawn not to males with the handsomest features or the best-proportioned bodies, but to those with the most authority, the fewer relatives in the unhappy event of inheritance disputes, and the smallest list of personal debts.

Thus, the boys had the better time of it by far. Since the mere sight of them was not assumed to be aphrodisiacal to the opposite sex, they were permitted, except on Sundays and in the wintertime, to expose a great deal more of healthy flesh to open air and water and summer breezes and the ripe sun-stricken languor of autumn afternoons than was ever possible for their contemporaries of the opposite sex.

For the girls, of course, *everything* was covered. In this respect I have often felt that our elders came as close to Purdah as they felt they could without provoking open rebellion. From the age of eleven to the day of their marriages the sight of bare female skin above the elbow or below the clavicle was so rare as to set young men's skin twitching for hours at a stretch. What made the matter even worse from the boy's point of view was the sight of each Monday morning's wash hanging from every clothesline in Forchheim—long black or white stockings, underpanties, garter belts, bloomers, beribboned petticoats, winter underwear, laced corslets, dresses, skirts, flour sacks cut and sewn into four-inch padded squares with tie-cords attached, which were understood to serve the most erotic purposes imaginable—all of these feminine secrets were displayed, even flaunted, before our yearning eyes fifty-two times a year, and yet what they touched each day as a matter of casual necessity we were forbidden to touch or even think about without risking spiritual perdition and sometimes physical assault of the most brutal sort.

It was not at all uncommon for a young man to be almost famished with the desire to touch the tip of his finger to a girl's cheek and still not dare to, even though he knew that the underpanties she wore were either white with little pink ribbons, pink with white polka dots, blue with lace edges, or pale yellow with elastic bands, and that her menstrual cycle had ended three days before.

Thus, at fifteen, I was a virgin, and so was Gunther Blobel and most others of our age with the possible exception of the nobility, who were reputed to have their pleasure not only of barmaids and servant girls, but often of girls of their own class.

For the rest of us, however, this widespread plague of adolescent male virginity naturally brought out the worst in our incurably carnal natures. Instead of treating girls as objects of desire (or at least of consideration) we tormented them unmercifully, dipped the tips of their blond braids into inkwells, crept after school hours into their toilets to decorate their walls with lewd doggerel and obscene drawings, arranged for occasional dribbles of water to appear on the floor beneath their classroom chairs, cribbed shamelessly from their examination papers despite their vindictive efforts—elbows outspread on their desks like the wings of brooding hens—to conceal their work from our craning necks and spying eyes.

And then, of course, we masturbated.

Today, the young people I watch from my front stoop are entirely different, both in attire and, I am convinced, in their sexual relations with each other. God knows, with the Russians breeding like cats on one side of us and the French like rabbits on the other, the more sound German breeders we can raise the more secure our fate will be in years to come.

I go into such detail about sexual practices among those of my age in a time which seems already passing into ancient history to emphasize that there *was* a difference between then and now, and that one cannot possibly pass fair judgment upon either the present or the past without at least a beginner's knowledge of what the past was like.

It also explains, I think, the extraordinary sexual experience which befell Gunther and me on that first magical night at Hoher Meissner—an experience I shall never regret nor forget as long as I live.

AUTHOR'S NOTE

In Chapter 10 (which is unfinished), amidst the dying campfires and fading songs atop Hoher Meissner, Grieben seduces

Gunther in what will be the only homosexual experience of his life—although not of Gunther's.

THE SEDUCTION OF GUNTHER: FRAGMENTS INTENDED FOR CHAPTER 10

A thousand campfires glowed that night on Hoher Meissner, more than ever before, we were told by those who had made the pilgrimage in earlier years; a thousand campfires and ten thousand wanderers and seekers and finders. After consuming our portion of *Schleim* from the community pots together with what bread and sausages we had stuffed into our duffel bags or abstracted from generous but unknowing peasants en route, we washed our utensils and ourselves in the pools and cataracts of the clear and swift-flowing mountain stream called "Tears of the Virgin," which descended the northern side of the mountain in its tumultuous passage to the river Main; and then the real purpose of our convocation got under way.

A mist had begun to diffuse what an hour earlier had been the sure brilliance of an autumn moon while farther out—millions and billions and trillions of light years into time—a sparkling of silver had already dusted the luminescence of more distant galaxies with celestial trash, which since the beginning of time had circled the moon's gigantic orb until man, with the simple pinch of thumb and forefinger, had reduced it in a fit of mathematical madness to the size of a mummified pigmy.

It was I who brought up the subject, not Gunther.

"Do you remember that afternoon in the woods outside Forchheim?"

"What afternoon?" he asked.

"With Inge."

"Sure I remember."

"Pretty, wasn't she?"

"She sure was."

"Yeah. With the hair just beginning to grow between her legs. It was so soft. Do you know something?"

"What?"

"I used to put my hand between her legs before there was any hair there at all. Just soft white skin with that little slit up the middle of it."

"If we had done it to her that afternoon do you think it would have hurt her?"

"*Hurt* her! Of course not! I used to stick my finger up her cunt clear to here. Her tits would get hard as little rocks. She would wiggle like it was tickling her and move her bottom up and down and pant like she had been running. Do you think she would do it if it was hurting her? Of course not! She loved it. They all do. Although they have to pretend differently, they *want* us to fuck them. They think of getting fucked as much as we think of fucking them!"

"Were you fucking Inge all that while? I mean before she had any hair growing there at all up to the afternoon when you took her pants off?"

"Of course."

The lie, which by now I had to make, sent a stab of regret through my heart, so poignant that I felt nothing but gratitude for the darkness of night that dulled the moisture which suddenly filled my eyes.

ALTERNATE BEGINNING

A thousand campfires glowed that night on Hoher Meissner, more than ever before, we were told by those who had made the pilgrimage before; a thousand campfires and ten thousand wanderers and seekers and finders. A pallid crescent moon hung high in the eastern sky while above it and farther out, millions and billions and trillions of light years into time, a sprinkling of silver had already begun to dust the luminescence of more distant galaxies with celestial trash.

Far below and to the north gleamed the lights of Kassel, to which the first emperor of the new German Reich had sent Napoleon III after the French defeat at Sedan. To the south a glimmering trail of isolated farm lights traced the wandering course of the Fulda. From the dark side of the forest [. . .] the light from a woodcutter's hut.

◆

"Do you think we will always be friends as we are now?"

"Of course. Why not?"

"Things change. People change. Friends change."

"We don't."

"Do you remember Inge?"

"Of course. What do you mean?"

"How just before she ran away you told her you were going to let me touch her anywhere I wanted to? I mean, after her clothes were off?"

"Sure I remember."

"Would you have let me?"

"Sure."

"Why?"

"Because—we are friends. If I could touch her, why shouldn't you be able to?"

"Do you think she would let me?"

"She'd have had to, if she hadn't run away."

"I don't know."

(NOTE BY TRUMBO: *A thought—then the pre-play begins, ultimately connection.*)

◆

Paul and Karl had separated from us long ago. Fenri had stayed beside the council fire of the Youth Brotherhood. Gunther and I had made a bed of pine branches, spread our blankets, and left our rucksacks and most of our clothes beside it.

Part II

TRUMBO'S SYNOPSIS

♦ I ♦

Grieben and the Rise of the Third Reich

In the last year of the war Ludwig Grieben, at the age of seventeen, joins the Bavarian Army, together with his friend, Gunther Blobel. They are part of what the Germans called the Children's Brigades, which drew off and slaughtered the last available reservoir of young German manhood. The generation immediately preceding having been wiped out, only boys were left to fill the reserve units of the tottering German Empire. They were trained in six weeks and rushed into combat with inadequate equipment against Allied forces that were steadily increasing in numbers, strength, and firepower. Result: They were killed or maimed by the hundreds of thousands.

When they march proudly to the front, Ludwig and Gunther, like all of their contemporaries, are drunk with the glory of war, with the myth of inevitable German victory, with adoration of the God-Emperor who (as they presumed) stood at the forefront of the struggle and had (as they were told) moved his person and imperial headquarters from Berlin and Potsdam to the front so that the Supreme War Lord could live in closer communion with his men. In the East the Russian autocracy had collapsed, the Treaty of Brest-Litovsk had added tens of thousand of hectares to the Greater Germany and, at least to the uninitiated, there was glory to be won, a nation of heroes to be birthed. To German youth it was *still* the most romantic of wars.

What they find when they reach the front is something quite different: the energetic stupidity of Ludendorff, the massive imperturbability of Hindenburg, the hysterical uncertainty of Wilhelm II, the murderous fool's vanity of his Crown Prince; the average strength of a battalion sunk to 660 to 665 men; food, clothing, transport, artillery and even ammunition in short supply. What they find, in short, is mud, hunger, deprivation, blood, and death.

As the army reels back from the American breakthrough in the Argonne and begins its vast general retreat toward the boundaries of the German homeland, the military atmosphere turns acrid with the stench of death and defeat. It is those bitter years of 1917–1918 which conditioned a whole generation of German youth, the controlling generation of the future, for revolution: revolution from the right, revolution from the left, revolution from below or above, but in any and every event—revolution.

In the midst of it all they read a news dispatch: "This evening His Majesty returned from Avesnes bursting with the news of our success. To the guard on the platform he shouted as the Imperial Train pulled in: 'The battle is won, the English have been utterly defeated.' There was champagne for dinner. A communiqué was prepared telling of our great victory under the personal leadership of His Majesty the Emperor. . . ."

The preconditions for revolution which prepare Grieben and Blobel for the lives they are to lead, as well as Klaus Winterfeld and Helmuth Morgen, their two closest comrades-in-arms, were these:

1. Complete separation of the officers corps, with its inherited privileges, from the foot soldier who had no privileges at all.

2. The alienation of the aristocracy from the newly risen class of bourgeois industrialists and mercantile bankers who were charged with enriching themselves while the army bled to death.

3. The alienation of front-line soldiers from the aristocracy, the bourgeoisie, and even from workers and peasants on the home front.

4. The abject surrender of the Reichstag to Imperial authority, and the complete inability of the Emperor and his court to lead, move forward, retreat, or even govern.

5. News reaching the front (mostly in letters from families or friends or those returned from home leave) of deprivation, hunger, bankruptcy, stagnation, and disintegration.

6. Disloyalty in the ranks, covert violence against the officer corps, revolutionary agitation, even mutiny.

7. The defeat of German allies in the East; the loss of conquered provinces, even conquered nations—Bulgaria, Greece, most of what is now Yugoslavia, Albania, Montenegro; the rout of the Turks; rumors of the impending Austro-Hungarian defection.

8. The overwhelming (and steadily growing) superiority of the Anglo-French-American coalition in the West; the agony and slaughter of the stubborn German retreat; the adamant refusal of the Western Powers to offer any terms but capitulation; the (by now) obvious certainty of German defeat.

9. The presence in the East of a Russian government which has placed world revolution on its agenda, thereby arousing fear and hostility in the propertied and peasant classes, and romantic hope in many in the working class who stood on the brink of abandoning the Social Democratic Party, which to now had claimed most of their loyalties, in favor of new groups and organizations which advocated open and immediate and violent revolutionary action.

Such are the conditions in which Ludwig Grieben, Gunther Blobel, Klaus Winterfeld, and Helmuth Morgen fight their war for the glory of the Fatherland and the honor of their Emperor. In the course of that last year of butchery and betrayal, Morgen becomes a revolutionary (and will die a Communist); Blobel falls violently in love with Winterfeld (a tall, fair, slender youth with the eyes of an angel and the soul of a bad poet)—an affair that Grieben at first threatens to denounce to his superiors but later accepts with no diminution of his comradely affection for his boyhood chum; while Grieben himself kills five Frenchmen and two Senegalese in hand-to-hand combat, murders his captain (a fool, a martinet, and a count) by a shot in the back on a dark night, twice wins the Iron Cross, and emerges from the war (a) loveless and (b) a loner.

That portion of the novel dealing with the experiences of our characters in actual combat will be much shorter than the outline indicates. World War I itself has been more than adequately dealt with in fiction. It is important to the novel only in the degree to which it has formed a very young and ongoing generation for whom defeat has destroyed every value, every reality, every moral standard, which they were trained to accept, without offering them anything to replace it.

Thus, unlike the English or the French or the Russians, each of whom shed as much or even more blood than their principal enemy, the Germans of eighteen to twenty who survived the slaughter emerged from the Army into a world quite unlike that of their Western contemporaries—a world conditioned by defeat, violent revolutionary ferment, economic collapse, unemployment, the wildest kind of inflation, and the geographical accident which made their country a buffer between the revolutionary East and an increasingly counterrevolutionary West.

Denied any hope of education beyond the minimal level they had achieved before entering the Army, rootless, propertyless, declassed, unemployed, hating the aristocracy who had failed them, the bourgeoisie who had exploited them, the intellectuals who had betrayed them, and the new government which represented all three of their enemies, large numbers of them emerge from the armed forces as freebooters—angry, cynical, frustrated, vengeful men, eager to dispossess others as they themselves had been dispossessed, ready to use anything—fists, knives, clubs, guns—for the destruction of a society they despise, crying out for a leader—*any* leader—who will identify their faceless enemy and point the way to his destruction.

For a full decade the divided world powers watch Germany's agony with bated breath: would the left prevail over the right, or the right over the left? The country was flooded with spies, agents, money, trade agreements, treaties, arms until at long last the decision made itself apparent. The road to victory lay on the right. Christendom sighed with relief and thanked God.

Thus Hitler, the Nazi Party, the Third Reich, salvation from the great pestilence to the East, and justice for the Jew.

The personal stories which comprise the novel are these:

The homosexual relationship between Blobel and Winterfeld, which begins in the trenches, comes to Grieben as a profound emotional shock, since to him it represents the loss of another love. Only when he understands Blobel's infatuation with Winterfeld as comparable to that of a man for a woman is he able to forgive him and return to their former relationship as friends and comrades.

In the last days of the war, Winterfeld is totally blinded by premature explosion of a star shell. Blobel is desolated, not only by the tragedy itself, but by their physical separation while Winterfeld is hospitalized. Grieben and Morgen console him: by the time their unit is dismantled and its members dismissed, the three have become inseparable companions.

They emerge into a German Republic wracked by hunger and revolution. Morgen goes to Munich where he joins the Red Front in support of the new Social Democratic government under Kurt Eisner and engages in the first street fights with units of the Socialist Workers Party, forerunner of the NSDAP.

Grieben and Blobel join one of the many *Freikorps*—small private armies of freebooters secretly armed by the Reischswehr from hidden arsenals. They roam the disputed areas of Silesia and the Baltic and Polish borders, robbing, plundering, raping, killing— all in the name of the Fatherland and its defenseless frontiers. The victors have limited the Reichswehr to 100,000 soldiers: the response is 100,000, 200,000, 300,000 armed men, working sometimes with the Army, sometimes against it, but never *of* it—a ruthless revolutionary or counterrevolutionary force, sometimes for hire, sometimes not, and never under the control of national or provincial authorities. They rage through Thuringia and Hamburg fighting the Spartacists, infiltrate the Ruhr valley to harass French occupation forces, and sometimes sweep down on private enemies for private vengeance. It is a good life for young men who have no hope of a permanent home or steady employment: uniforms, food, lots to drink, lots of girls, hearty German comradeship and a little plunder.

In May of 1919, in conjunction with the army, they move against the newly established Bavarian Soviet Republic in Munich, overthrow it and engage in a general massacre. It is Grieben's firing squad which, to his and Blobel's horror, is assigned the task of executing Helmuth Morgen. They loathe the job, but they carry it through as good fellows must.

Their Freikorps is absorbed into the Ehrhardt Brigade, which marches on Berlin in March, 1920, and there, while the Reichswehr stands aside and the government flees to the west, installs Wolfgang Kapp as Chancellor and putative dictator. Only a general strike restores the republican government to power.

A year later, still in the madhouse of postwar Berlin, Grieben and Blobel hear Adolf Hitler speak for the first time, and lose both their hearts and their heads to him. They abandon the undisciplined life of the Freikorps to join first the Nazi Party, and then the Sturmabteilung, or SA, under the command of Goering and Captain Ernst Roehr.

In 1923 Blobel discovers Winterfeld, his blind eyes concealed behind dark glasses, playing the piano in a homosexual nightclub patronized almost exclusively by industrialists, foreign diplomats, and the Reichswehr elite. They immediately resume their old relationship.

Although his days are filled with SA activities and street brawls, Grieben, deprived in the evenings of Blobel's company, grows lonely. He thinks of Inge. He thinks of Morgen, murdered and buried in Munich. He thinks of Blobel and Winterfeld. He meets, courts, and marries a young woman two years older than himself, not because he loves her but because he is depressed and lonely. Also she has inherited a small house completely free of encumbrance.

It is a time in which the mark was 75 to the dollar in 1921, 400 in 1922, 18,000 in January of 1923, 160,000 on July 1, a million on August 1, four billion in November and into the trillions before New Year's Day of 1924. To acquire not only a wife but a decent debt-free house in the Berlin of 1923 is a much larger piece of financial luck than it seems.

His wife presents him with two children in quick succession—children he doesn't very much want but doesn't actually dislike since he spends most of his time in the streets with SA comrades brawling for control of strategic corners, breaking up opposition political rallies, and prowling the industrial districts for striking workers. The easy communal barracks of the SA are pleasant places to be—almost clubs—with rallies and beer and music by night and always the sport of catching a few Jews or Communists or Social Democrats unwary enough to walk the night streets with only one or two of their kind for protection.

As Grieben's wife conceives and delivers his two children, as Berlin becomes the hunting ground for sexual exotics and political quacks from all over the world, as the sharp satire of cafés and nightclubs slowly changes (with, of course, changing personnel) to timid orthodoxy, as elections wax and wane, as the enfeebled Weimar Republic stumbles toward the grave (although not the undertaker) it so richly deserves, Ludwig Grieben advances from

Rottenfuehrer in the SA to Scharfuehrer and finally, in 1932, to Hauptscharfuehrer. His advance is neither swift nor very high. It is the advance of an ordinary man who believes in his profession and tries hard to learn it.

He begins to delve into German philosophy (always a murky and dangerous enterprise), into German history (even more dangerous and far less informative), and into political science as exemplified by the works of Hitler, Rosenberg, Goebbels, Haushofer, Anton Drexler, Houston Stewart Chamberlain, and the like. From these sources and close study of the Party press, he comes to certain rather shrewd conclusions about the future of the SA under the command of Ernst Roehm as opposed to that of the SS under the command of Heinrich Himmler. He resigns from the SA and applies for admission to the SS, which he enters late in 1932, with the rank of Untersturmfuehrer in a Guards unit of the Schutzstaffel later to be incorporated into the Death's-Head Formations of Himmler's reorganized security forces.

In the same year, resplendent in his new SS uniform, he also falls desperately in love with Liesel Dahlem, a young and extremely beautiful ballet dancer—not ballerina—in the Berlin Opera: She is attracted to him, but at the same time shy, perhaps even afraid, when she is with him. He begs her to sleep with him; she refuses. He begs her to become his mistress; she refuses. He begs his wife for a divorce; she refuses. Through the fading of 1932 and the political campaigns of 1933 (which begin with the national boycott of Jewish shops and reach their brilliant climax in the March elections with a Nazi victory, Hitler's *legal* ascension to the Chancellory, and the death of the Weimar Republic), Grieben's political passions, though strong and effective, are nothing compared with a passion for Liesel which is far stronger and maddeningly less effective.

He is with Liesel on the night of May 10, 1933, when tens of thousands of students, carrying torches and singing the *Horst Wessel*, march down the Unter den Linden to a rendezvous opposite the University of Berlin, and there consign to kerosine and torch every book which, by definition of the students' resolution, "acts subversively on our future or strikes at the root of German thought, the German home and the driving forces of our people."

The flames ... the dancing torches ... the chants ... the shouts ... the songs. Youth everywhere, boys, girls, SS, SA, fresh, rose-tinged cheeks, strong backs, tireless legs—the sounds and smells and movements of an emotional explosion almost orgiastic in its fusion of flesh with ideology. And Liesel beside him, clinging to his arm, shrinking against him, afraid of this splendid sight, needing his protection.

Grieben skillfully separates her from the crowd, takes her to a small park within sight and sound of the book-burning, and rapes her. Like all of his attempts at love, even rape is a failure. In that flash-second before penetration he ejaculates prematurely and merely soils her. While he is still trying, in his shame, to explain and apologize for what he defines as the curse of excessive virility, she springs to her feet and vanishes; vanishes not only from his sight but from the opera, from her rooms, from the places in which she once ate, from her friends, from Berlin, perhaps from the world. Years will pass before he sees her again.

FROM TRUMBO'S NOTE ON LIESEL

The instant falling in love with Liesel onstage (he progresses from balcony to orchestra at great cost), convinced that onstage she is looking and responding to him.

The idiotic fantasy of instant love—and first.

◆

Use expression such as "He *requires* to fall in love ..." etc.

♦

In the course of his infatuation with Liesel, his new treatment of his wife. No more underpants. Her pussy must always be available to his touch, his hand. The first thing he comes home. Anytime. And even once in church. Never in front of the children, of course. Can't [. . .].

And she liked it. It gave her pleasure. And like a good German girl she understood she must always be instantly available to love. To him, who is her master. *To him* really—not me, but him. His whim enmeshed both. She knelt before him, caressed him with her [. . .] soft hand, her cheek, kissed his blazing fountain and drank.

Scrap of a letter from his wife telling how in the past months his love (sensual) has flowered and grown and quite engulfed her in this different flood of love she feels for him. (This, of course, is while he is meeting and courting Liesel, who will have nothing to do with him.)

♦

Her small size. 95 pounds. Five feet, two inches. She says she is afraid. He thinks it is because of the size of his penis. His new uniform (SS) tight and black he dresses to the left. He has admired the bulge there. He has seen women look at the bulge. So that, he says, it is what she is afraid of. He tears her pants off, crouches on his knees above her, his knees between her outspread legs. His right hand on her buttock, the index and third fingers of his left hand spread her vulva while his second finger explores the trimness of her entrance hole, the shy covering of the clitoris; he thrusts gently inward, she protests, he soothes her, reassures her, explains to her, forces her hand to his penis, explains how he will insert the head first, very gently—she will stretch, in a week she will accommodate him perfectly—then as the head of his penis touches the moisture he showers her, pumping frantically, left groin, right groin, crack of her buttocks [. . .] the *mons veneris*—horror—disgust—she is covered with glue—she flees.

♦

June 30, 1934. The Night of the Long Knives. The final consolidation of Hitler's power over the SA, the Army, the church, the great industrialists—over everyone. With Himmler's SS in charge of the operation and Hitler personally participating in it, many old scores are settled in addition to the total liquidation of SA leadership. Roehm, the SA commander, is dragged from his bed in the Hanslbauer Hotel in Wiessee and shot. So are his companions, many of them homosexuals on leave with their lovers.

All over Germany, in every one of its major cities, men and sometimes women are aroused from sleep and dragged before the execution squads. Of more than a thousand who are to die this night, over 150 are SA men rounded up in Berlin for summary execution against a wall of the Cadet School at Lichterfelde—among then Gunther Blobel and Klaus Winterfeld.

Untersturmfuehrer Ludwig Grieben, firing squad command three, has tried to warn them earlier in the night, but they were not in their rooms. His secret instructions have made it clear that real or alleged homosexuality will stand high on the list of crimes which will be used to justify tonight's slaughter.

Now, as they appear in the corridor, arms tied behind their backs, hurried on their way by booted Death's-Head guards, Grieben takes refuge in the shadows of a recessed doorway and watches their approach—Gunther Blobel, the mortician's son from Forchheim, friend of his childhood years, wartime comrade, Freikorps and SA brother, his oldest and dearest friend: Klaus Winterfeld, delicate as a child, whose only crimes have been to dream of writing better poetry than his talents permit, and of loving illegally and being illegally loved in return.

As they pass his secret hiding place, Grieben can hear the moans which escape from Klaus's lips, and Gunther's gruff yet oddly gentle voice offering consolation; he can see Klaus's face, rigid with terror, and Gunther's filled with compassion and concern—concern not merely for himself but for someone else, for another.

Seeing Gunther thus, and hearing his voice, Grieben suddenly remembers a summer afternoon, a forest, a young girl, and Gunther saying, "Don't hurt her. . . ."

The vision passes. The corridor is empty. From the killing wall sharp commands can be heard, then a scream even sharper, then the merciful crash of rifle fire. It is over.

The squirrel. The doe rabbit. Inge. Helmuth Morgen. Liesel. Klaus Winterfeld. Gunther Blobel. Love and death. Love first and then death. Always and always and always . . .

The killer?

I! Ludwig Grieben! *I'm* the killer!

Why?

Because I love!

Slowly Grieben climbs the ladder of command. Special training, Death's-Head Formation. Dachau. Bergen-Belsen. Buchenwald. And then, as the war rushes to its insane climax, Auschwitz-Birkenau, at the third level of command.

Grieben lives with his wife and teen-age children in a cottage outside the camp—a cottage staffed by Jehovah's Witnesses, the most unconvinced but also the most obedient of the camp's inmate groups. A cottage with flower and vegetable gardens, fertilized each week by the materials he brings home from the camp—fertilizers which produce gigantic flowers and three-kilo turnips. Even the camp's great smokestacks, which day and night becloud the sky, sprinkle the hop vines beside his cottage door with a gentle residue that nourishes their vital functions and impels them to larger and much greener growth than vines from the same seeds planted only ten miles distant.

By day Grieben stolidly, earnestly pursues his chosen patriotic task of extermination.

♦ 2 ♦

Grieben's Diary

What follows are selections from approximately forty pages of the diary which, with others, will be interspersed from Chapter 11 of the novel to its end. D.T.

18 May 1939

Since 1933 we have been saying to the rest of the world, "If you're so concerned about the fate of our Jews, take them off our hands, they're all yours, they won't cost you anything, they're absolutely free. Take the whole lot of them and settle them wherever you wish—Madagascar, Africa, Alaska, Palestine—we don't care, all we want is to be rid of them."

Every time we have said it, something strange has happened. Yesterday, for example, England announced that the total Jewish population of Palestine must be held to one third that of the Arabian population; and that, in consequence, Jewish immigration to Palestine will be limited to a total of 75,000 Yidischer over the next five years: 15,000 Jews a year—and we have over 800,000 of them waiting for a place to go to!

Having watched the rest of the world's statesmen in speech and action for more than six years since this particular crisis threatened, I am more convinced than ever that Adolf Hitler is the only honest head of state on earth. The others may not agree with what he says, but as to forthright statement of future intentions they have not yet caught him in a lie.

I pledge my honor on a prediction that they never will.

6 August 1939

Goebbels keeps a sharp eye on the American press, which is filled with Jewish atrocity propaganda, and publishes his findings almost daily in *Der Angriff*. Some time ago a piece of legislation called the Child Refugee Bill was introduced in their Congress. It proposed to admit into the United States ten thousand German (read "Jewish") children under the age of fourteen during the present year, and another ten thousand in 1940, their migration to be supervised by a religious group called the American Friends Service Committee.

Today's *Der Angriff* tells what happened. A man named Kinnicutt, president of the Allied Patriotic Societies, which were said to include the New York County organizations of the American Legion, the American Women Against Communism, the Dames of the Loyal Legion, the Veterans of Foreign Wars, the United Daughters of the Confederacy, the Daughters of the Defenders of the Republic, the Society of Mayflower Descendants, the Sons of the American Revolution, the Daughters of the American Revolution, and the Lords' Day Alliance of the United States, attacked the proposed legislation on the grounds that "most of those to be admitted would be of the Jewish race." A Mrs. Waters of the Widows of World War I Veterans denounced the idea of admitting "thousands of motherless, embittered, persecuted children of undesirable foreigners." The Ladies of the Grand Army of the Republic called on the women of America to "arise and defend their own children." Other organizations which opposed the legislation were the Colonial Order of the Acorn, the American Vigilant Intelligence Federation, the Order of Colonial Lords of Manors in America, and the Defenders of the Constitution.

The law didn't pass. Julius Streicher published a very funny cartoon about it in *Der Stuermer*. The Americans don't want Jew kids any more than we do—and for the same reasons!

AUTHOR'S NOTE

Two diary entries immediately preceding the German invasion of the U.S.S.R.   D.T.

28 May 1941

Have been in Pretzsch, Saxony (near Leipzig), for three days now. We are, in all, just over one hundred junior officers sworn to absolute secrecy, ordered here for what has been described as a special training course that will take from three to four weeks, and billeted in Frontier Police School barracks. About a third of our number have served in the Government General of the Polish territories rounding up dissident intellectuals (including priests), sanitizing the larger ghetto areas, and resettling Jews. The rest of us have been detached from SS duty in France, Holland, Belgium, Denmark, Norway, the Protectorate of Bohemia, or the Reich itself.

The importance of whatever it is we are to be trained for may be judged by the Party standing of certain persons who are participating in the project at the highest level, and who *may* become our leaders, although nothing so specific as actual leadership of an actual enterprise has yet been hinted at: Erich von dem Bach-Zalewski, for example, not to mention such senior SS officers as Franz Jaeckeln, Otto Ohlendorf, Otto Rasch, Artur Nebe, Erich Naumann and Franz Stahlecker. We *do* know, however, that the project has been initiated by direct order of Obergruppenfuehrer and Police-General Reinhard Heydrich, which means, ultimately, Reichsfuehrer-SS Himmler himself. I consider my selection for whatever duties may be imposed upon me here to be the greatest honor thus far in my career.

29 May 1941

We are completely isolated here. Incoming and outgoing mail is censored. The telephone is forbidden. No contact with outsiders—not even local service personnel—is permitted. An order has just been received for the surrender of all writing materials—portable typewriters, pens, pencils, paper—as well as certificates of identification, personal papers, diaries and journals. Even Party cards! Everything will be returned to us, of course, but I have the strangest feeling that what they confiscate from us in this world will be returned to us in a world that is new and altogether different.

AUTHOR'S NOTE

Immediately after the preceding entry, they learn that the invasion of the USSR is at hand, and that they are to form four Einsatzgruppen whose tasks will be to operate immediately behind the Wehrmacht and SS rounding up and exterminating Jews, Communists, guerillas, and "unreliable elements." Grieben is assigned to Einsatzgruppe B, whose ultimate assignment is to police the city of Moscow. The following diary entries are made during his service with Einsatzgruppe B.   D.T.

13 August 1941

There are a number of reasons why these Jews are so easy to round up and kill:

1. Having lived within yet apart from the host populations on which they prey, they have developed a strong sense of social organization. In time of emergency, they will invariably do what their most respected leaders tell them to do. Thus by skillful manipulation of local leaders we are able to control and dictate the activities of an entire community.

2. They are obsessed with family loyalty. No emergency can induce them to abandon their aged, their infirm, or their chil-

dren. Youthful members of the community, who are always the strongest, most active, and hence most capable of escaping and fending for themselves, invariably remain with their families, which means, quite naturally, that they share the family fate. With them, of course, dies the best breeding stock.

3. For centuries the European Jew has lived as a social parasite outnumbered by his host population in a ratio of one or two hundred to one. Because the use of violence to achieve his ends would have resulted in immediate and overwhelming retaliation, he has survived (and prepared!) by means of secrecy, treachery, subversion, racial defilement, bribery, acquiescence, physical submission, etc., etc. It follows that he is fundamentally non-violent, hence completely incapable of resorting to organized physical resistance, or even individual personal defense.

4. For thousands of years the Jew has been taught, as an article of personal, racial, and religious faith, to *endure*, and through endurance to *survive*. Throughout his long history it has worked: i.e., by enduring he *has* survived. Such a philosophy, carried to the extreme as it has been by Jews, becomes not a philosophy but a fact of life: i.e., *if* you endure, you *will* survive. Because of this they cannot believe—indeed, they find it inconceivable—that we intend to exterminate them as systematically as any other breed of disease-carrying vermin. Being unable to comprehend this fundamental fact, they endure us—i.e., obey our orders—as a necessary, though unpleasant, precondition for survival. Thus, at the last moment, when they discover the purpose of our game is not survival but extermination, it is too late for them to do anything but die.

28 September 1941

Driving through the village of . . . we passed eleven dead partisans dangling from a trestle gallows in front of temporary Wehrmacht Command Headquarters. Hands tied behind their backs, heads tilted forward as if in prayer, or leaning sideward as if in solemn attention to the next cadaver's words, they hung straight and still, as if frozen by the chill autumnal air. Three of them were women (one no more than 16) whose skirts had been torn off for reasons that did no honor to the Wehrmacht. However, their underwear was intact and still properly positioned, so there was nothing indecent about them except the stomach-turning ooze of death's incontinence seeping down their legs and, in the case of the girl (who obviously had been hanged on a full stomach), onto the earth below. We observed with interest that passing villagers—even the children—did not react in any way to the sight of their dead compatriots. Some, indeed, appeared not even to see them. There is a lack of human feeling in these Slavs I find it hard to understand.

I think I should note here that the victims' shoes had been removed and apparently taken from the area before execution, and that their bare or sock-covered feet had been chopped off just above the ankle joints. Three or four of the severed feet still remained where they had fallen. Fifty yards down the road a surly mongrel gnawing at the remains of a human foot told us what had happened to the rest. Lieutenant Richter, with whom I rode, has decided to report this public example of Wehrmacht sadism to [. . .]. It is hard enough for us of the SS to deal with these people as duty compels us to: it is not permissible to enjoy or make a public spectacle of it.

18 October 1941

It goes on and on and on, each of us participating, each taking his turn at the gun so that none will feel more "innocent," less "guilty," than his comrades. We have all been driven mad in one degree or another. Yet no amount of schnapps (we drink shocking amounts, all of us, we have to) can dull the knowledge that even as we swore our oaths we *knew* it would be this way. We few—there were never more than four thousand men in all the Einsatzgruppen—have accepted in behalf of the German race a burden of horrors so awful that they cannot even be dreamed of without a howl, a rage for death, a loosening of the bowels, a creeping mantle of shit to hide the rubies and brightly burning diamonds of Jerusalem.

Yet, as I say, we knew from the beginning that it would be so: Himmler himself told us at the outset. Only by remembering his words do I prevent myself from going mad:

It is easier to lead a company into battle than to deport people, to remove shrieking, weeping women, to carry out executions. When a unit covers itself with glory in battle, that can be talked about openly and the unit can be suitably rewarded. But for you to do this unseen duty, to maintain this silent activity, to be at all times the consistent and uncompromising guardian of our ideology, to commit day after day such frightful deeds that even in our inmost circles we cannot really speak of them, and to carry the secret of all you have done for the German race and Reich into the grave itself—that is a fate harder than death, more heroic than victory in open combat.

That is the burden I have *consciously* accepted. So be it. We have been here in Borisov since October 8. Central Army Group Headquarters were transferred to Smolensk two days ago, leaving the way much clearer for local action. The ghetto is organized. Tomorrow we move: one Sonderkommando, four hundred White Russian militia, and as many Ukrainian volunteers as we can use.

21 October 1941

Borisov, the accursed, has been cleansed. Its entire Jewish population—7,620 in all—went to the pits two days ago. It was like a dream. On they came to the killing ground, Jew after Jew after Jew, all of them naked as newborn children: skinny old men with beards; women with thick legs and stout, rolling, postmenopausal haunches; mothers herding their huddled, bare-skinned children; limp-penised fathers shamed by their helplessness; boys white as newly dug grubs; girls in bud with huge eyes, if right-handed covering genitals with their left, if left-handed with their right, the other clutching at tough little breasts—and *looking* at us—all of them looking at us as if we weren't there—or if there, weren't human, as if we were beasts—not recognizing that we, like them, are under orders; that we, like them, must obey and finally die; that we, like them, or perhaps *un*like them, are also human beings.

I saw a father moving in the front ranks toward the pit. I saw a little boy break free from his mother and thrust his way through those naked marching bodies crying "Wait for me, Father—wait for me!" And the father waited, and the boy arrived at his side, and the father took the boy's hand, and they walked together. Toward what? Toward death. Why?

Well behind the father and son a pale, knob-jointed, speckle-skinned, blue-veined old man, revolting in his nakedness, really indecent, his scrotum a doughy crepe bag, bare, bald, truly obscene, yet swinging lower than his dangling penis—he presses forward with the anxious, urgent eyes of an old dog, turns and twists through the crowd like a demented goat crying "Wait for me! Wait for me!"

The father and son wait. The naked old horror catches up with them. Hand in hand they arrive at the lip of the pit and turn their backs to it and look straight at the guns. Why don't their eyes search instead for a wife, a child, a mother? Or is it really possible to separate one's own from someone else's in this dense-packed seeping clot of Jewesses, each like every other in despair and weeping nakedness?

The guns bark. Father, son, and old bald-balls fall backward into the pit. The women arrive feeling they are not themselves because for the first time, naked and together, they *are* themselves. They turn to face the guns, nervously arranging their silent, ox-eyed offspring in the proper order, eager that the children give no one any trouble, that they draw no attention to themselves through misbehavior, that they give evidence of their humanity by accepting death with a decorum it was not possible for them to manifest in that other traumatic instant when, quite involuntarily, they were made to accept life.

Questions. Questions and questions and questions.

In those last seconds of life, why didn't the doomed men at the pit's edge lift their eyes even once for a last glimpse of their lost and moaning women? Because suddenly the women were *all*, they were everything, they were earth and sun and sky and life, and the men were nothing and ashamed of their nothingness, and they could not bear to look once more on the blinding beauty it had been their life's most urgent duty to protect. With manhood one can look at anything; deprived of it, at nothing except that nothing that comes as death from the barrel of a gun.

And because the women were concerned with propriety and the decent conduct of their children, they, too, did not look away from the task at hand, nor bestow a single glance on their dying men.

Oh God, it's true, there is no escaping from its truth. Those naked, fretting, dying Jewesses actually thought that if we saw how nicely their children behaved, how sweet and intelligent and loving and beautiful they truly were, we would not kill them! One child—may his soul be blasted from God's memory—one child no more than five, it seemed—it was a boy, I think, although at such times no one can be sure—this one Satanic, Christ-abandoned child lifted his hand—his left hand, I remember it clearly—it was only a split-second before his face disintegrated—he lifted his left hand and smiled and waved farewell—at *me!*

Why me? It wasn't *my* bullet that struck him. The movement of his hand caught my eye and sent my bullet wide. The body slowly, reluctantly, lingeringly tumbled backward into the pit—tumbled like a stunned animal, like a squirrel, perhaps. But it was not my gun that did him in.

The whole thing, of course, was an accident. That I freely admit to be the truth. Yet *because* it was an accident I neither killed the child nor disobeyed my orders. That was a good moment in my life. They *do* come sometimes, don't they? More than a good moment, it was one of the best. Hail Mary! Gloria in excelsis!

The boy, of course, looking straight at the barrel of the gun with my face behind it, had no way of knowing it was not I who blew the light from his eyes and the smile from his face and scattered his brains like sewage over the weedy grass and fresh-dug earth. No matter. When you have walked as far as I have across earth turned by fresh blood and warm brains into mire, into soft-sucking muck, into filth ankle-deep and almost (but not quite) as long as God's gut—and when, walking thus, you have heard, as one hears a distant wind, the rushing of souls, thousands of souls, the anguish of their search, the murmur of their passage, now here, now there, it was all so sudden, we weren't prepared, have we lost anyone, I didn't think it would be like this, the grayness, the chill, infinity is too large, nothing should be without limits, our little house, my little room, the cow, the lock of hair from my grandfather's beard, where shall we go, where shall we rest again, when shall we sleep, are we old, are we young, are we real, what is left of us to be healed, to be helped, to be cared for, to be wanted, is that about me which made you love me still with me?

We must go now. Did they hurt you too much? I'm sorry. Never again will I let you be hurt. Never again will I let you be frightened. Take my hand. The mystery is here, and we must find it, but where is the light, where is the darkness, where is the Temple, the Torah, where is Jerusalem, where is God?

Gone. All gone. There is nothing here but the wind. We have become eternity. No, no, that can't be true, I just came from there. Forgive me, God, I had arrangements to make, I wasn't ready, I didn't finish, why must I go back so soon, why must I say goodbye?

Because I, Ludwig Richard Johann Grieben, have said that you must. What other answer can I give them? And how can I give it without hating them?

Because I *do* hate them. Their laments are an incitement, a provocation, a deliberately vengeful torment. No one who has watched them sink into their graves like slobbering animals can fail to recognize the calculated cruelty of their goodbyes, their farewells, their forever-and-ever-amens.

3 November 1941

Vitebsk. In the course of normal operations we trapped between 600 and 700 Jews at Saturday services in a ramshackle synagogue at the edge of the ghetto. Sealing all exits, we set the building afire on four sides and ringed the place with armed Ukrainian volunteers to make certain none could escape.

As those inside realized the terrible fate their god had prepared for them in the very heart of his temple, a great sob seemed to arise from within the building, a muted confusion of prayers and shrieks, of moaning and crying and wailing, of curses howled and bodies crashing vainly against stout oak doors that had been designed to prevent invaders from breaking in rather than worshippers from breaking out.

Listening to that remote and mindless cacophony, I found myself transported by memory once again to Forchheim as both it and I used to be in my youth. At the rear of my father's property there stood a small storage house built, at his order, of rock and structural concrete, one section of which, consisting of four hollow concrete blocks, had been infested by a colony of Vespa wasps. Their point of ingress and egress was a tiny break in the concrete no more than three centimeters across, through which those hungry, carnivorous insects with their great dangling legs passed in summer-long, two-way processionals.

There came a day when my father tired of his hymenopterous guests and, through me, arranged for their total destruction. At the end of a summer day, when twilight had brought the last wandering wasp to rest in some cell of his colony's impregnable concrete fortress, I, executioner of wasps and other creatures, poured a small vial of prussic acid into the fortress's sally port, sealed the hole with mud, pressed my ear to its still sun-warmed outer surface, and listened through an inch of solid concrete to the rising commotion from within, the muffled hum and buzz of a universe utterly consumed by the visible presence of death and its own terrible passion to live.

Listening there in the twilight, I could imagine the twitching of cocooned larvae, the waving heads of newborn grubs, the panic of nurses scurrying wildly from charge to charge, the frustrated rush of the workers for egress, the disorder of the guards, and beyond everything else the fierce agony of the queen, sovereign by now of all the dead and mother of the dying.

Such were my thoughts today in Vitebsk as the synagogue burned and the lamentations of those within it slowly ceased.

7 November 1941

Last night I dreamed that I stood face to face—no more than six inches between us—with a young woman, actually a girl, a girl I knew, a girl whom I seemed to have known years ago. Although I knew her in my dream and know her now, I can't remember who she was or is. She looked up at me and said, very softly, "Are we falling in love again?"

She couldn't have been Beata, who has the devotion of a spaniel and no capacity at all to fall in love. She couldn't have been Inge, whose sultry perfume I last inhaled in Forchheim seven years ago. And certainly she wasn't Liesel, who does not love me, did not love me, could not love me, will not love me, heaven and earth without end.

Did anyone ever truly fall in love with me? I think not. No one but her who came to me last night, her whom I cannot name but who is more real to me than life itself: "Are we falling in love again?"

The answer is yes. Fall in love with me, I beg you; fall in love with me again and again and again, remembering that for him who has loved you always it cannot possibly be again.

25 February 1942

The whole world has been given a chance to evaluate the sincerity of England's sympathy for Europe's "persecuted" Jews. The story, as it came out today, is this: between 700 and 800 Balkan and Ukrainian Jews, including seventy children, chartered a dilapidated 180-ton steamer (the *Struma*) to transport the lot of them from Constanza on the Black Sea to Palestine. The ship broke down off Istanbul. Since not one Jew aboard had immigration papers, the British, who already have more Jews in Palestine than any country really needs, refused to issue *navicerts* for them to proceed, and the Turks, of course, couldn't legally permit them to land.

For weeks, with the whole world watching, the *Struma* lay crippled in the Bosporus, her cargo sustained by various Jewish organizations in Istanbul. After two and a half months of this, the Turks had no choice but to tow the vessel out to sea, which, in full regard for international law, they did. Yesterday, six miles from shore, it sank. Only two of its 769 Jews had the wits or ability or strength to save themselves by swimming ashore.

Like any other man with human feelings I have had, and sometimes still do have, dark moments late at night while sleepless and alone, and particularly since the beginning of my work here with Einsatzkommando 4, in which I have pondered and even agonized over the justice of what we are doing and the necessity of doing it. Then, like a flash of lightning, one incident such as the sinking of the *Struma* illuminates the moral problem with blinding clarity: no country on earth wants these Jews we're risking our lives and souls to get rid of. *No country on earth.*

6 March 1942

Every time I haul my trousers up and look down into one of these filthy Russian toilets I see sausages stuffed with blood. Something inside me bleeds. I bleed in my belly. I bleed in my bowels. My asshole is like the cut throat of a Jew. Vodka, schnapps, brandy from France, hands full of aspirin, Seconal, Nembutal, codeine, opium. There are different flavors here. There is a new kind of death. My life is a scum.

20 March 1942

From London: After questions in the House of Commons three days ago about the sinking of the Jew ship *Struma,* the Undersecretary for the Colonies, a Mr. Harold Macmillan, referred to the Palestine White Paper of 1939 and said, "It is not in our power to take measures of a nature that may compromise the present policy regarding illegal immigration."

How can the same man who tells the world that he and his government prefer to see Europe's rejected Jews rotting on the bottom of the sea rather than living in British-controlled Palestine turn around, as this man often has, and make propaganda speeches about "the inhuman racial policies of Nazi Germany?"

I vomit.

11 May 1942

More and more frequently I have this dream, which is really a dream within a dream: I am young again. I seem to be sleeping. And then, in my sleep, I hear his voice. For a moment the dream tells me that I hear him singing. His voice is high and pure. It is the voice of a girl, as boys' and young men's voices often are; yet sweeter than a girl's can ever be, more filled with yearning, more loving, far, far gentler.

I stir in my dream but I do not wake. The sweetness of his song turns somber; it is filled with melancholy, with longing, it is dark with reproach. It has become the voice of a man, richer now in its timbre, yet still sweet—sweet as an oboe and sadder. The song, which began as pure melody, now searches for words and finds them. The song is a question: *"Why? . . . Why? . . . why?"*

I start from my sleep. I am lying on a bed of pine needles deep in that same forest of perpetual midnight into which I was born—that dark and secret place toward which I have been stumbling all my life in order to die as secretly, as privately, as casually as a lizard when his belly shrivels and his trifocal eyes scum over and he summons his last strength to crawl back to the ancestral rock and the secret dust in which, safe at last, he can without shame cease reaching for air and stop being.

"Gunther," I cry, "where are you?" His voice replies, "I am dead." "So am I! I am dead too, Gunther!" Then, after a moment's silence, he responds. "Then come to me."

I jump to my feet in this dream within a dream. Although I am quite dry, I discover that the trees of the forest in which I have slept stand rooted in water. Beyond them, at the forest's edge, stretches a tarn. From the steely face of the tarn rises a mist, and there, where the mist swirls thickest, shimmering like a pale column risen from its depths, dripping tarn water and rotted rose petals, stands Gunther.

The water that stands beneath the trees parts for me as I run toward the tarn. I rush into its shallows through rising water and whirling mists until at last I am swimming beneath its iron-cruel surface, swimming like an eel through the very heart of it, gliding toward the white tower of all that I love until at last I cling to the rock on which he stands. I embrace the nakedness of his slim white feet; his toes so slender, so cold; his unridged nails so smooth, so firm, so young. I press my lips against the delicate hollow of his arches. I warm his skin with my kisses.

In that instant my dream becomes a memory. Midnight bonfires on the crest of Hoher Meissner blaze forth as midsummer greetings to the farms and vineyards below and the lights of Kassel blinking far to the north.

Gunther and I stand side by side once again, his arm around my waist, mine around his. We stand side by side and we are singing, singing together, thousands of us singing in one voice, singing on Hoher Meissner not for me-thou but for thou-me-us;

not for one but for all; not for cool heads but for hot hearts; not for the mass but for the one, the godlike one, the leader, the secret emperor—for that and the rare blue flower, forever shy, forever secret, forever holy.

Only six years before that fervid summer of 1913, in the course of which Gunther and I became closer than brothers can ever hope to be, Stefan George spoke for all of us when he cried that "*Volk* and high counsel yearn for The Man!—the *Deed!* . . . Perhaps someone who sat for years among your murderers and slept in your prisons will stand up and *do the deed!*"

That is what we were singing about that night amidst the campfires on Hoher Meissner; that is what we were singing about and waiting for. The Man, the Leader, the Secret Emperor, and the holy blue flower.

'Twas once—methinks year one of our blessed Lord—
Drink without wine, the Sybil thus deplored:—
"How ill things go!
Decline! Decline! Ne'er sank the world so low!
Rome now hath turned harlot and harlot-stew,
Rome's Caesar a beast, and God—hath turned Jew!"

I slept last night (and dreamed this dream for the fourth or fifth time) in Mogilev, where I am on temporary assignment to Sonderkommando 8 of my own Einsatzgruppe B.

AUTHOR'S NOTE

Almost immediately after the preceding entry Grieben suffers a nervous breakdown and is hospitalized.   D.T.

16 June 1942

Today they gave back my diary and writing materials. I asked for them when I first realized that I was a patient here (Base Hospital 64). That was on June 12, but my request was rejected as premature. They tell me I was flown here on May 14, but I have no recollection of it. I'm in the psychiatric ward.

Apparently I was found unconscious in Captain Golitzer's office on May 13 while assigned to Sonderkommando 8 in Mogilev, which means that from May 13 to June 12—almost a full month—I was not aware of my own existence, although they assure me that through the whole time I have led an apparently active conscious life. By that I mean that I seem to have awakened each morning and slept each night, but have no memory of it whatever. Apparently I was paralyzed part of the time, mostly on my right side. The only sign of it now is my right arm and hand. They are swollen and covered with rash, and the hand shakes a good deal. I am on a liquid diet for ulcers. They tell me the paralysis will clear up entirely. They are going to tell me more as my condition improves.

AUTHOR'S NOTE

After his breakdown with the Einsatzgruppe and his application for transfer, have him interviewed on his moral and political condition (anatomy of SS state), with the result that he is assigned to Auschwitz. All but the last of the following diary entries were written in Auschwitz.   D.T.

27 October 1943

Here is something to lighten the heart—a propaganda document called the Moscow Declaration just signed and published by Stalin, Churchill, and Roosevelt. In it the world is informed that "Germans who take part in the wholesale shooting of Italian officers or in the execution of French, Dutch, Belgian, or Norwegian hostages, or of Cretan peasants, or who have shared in slaughters inflicted on the people of Poland, or in the territories of the Soviet

Union which are now being swept clear of the enemy, will know that they will be brought back to the scene of their crimes and judged on the spot by the people whom they have outraged."

I have read this curious document with profound interest. I understand it perfectly. Indeed, I have memorized the whole statement. It speaks of Italians, French, Dutch, Belgians, Norwegians, Cretans, Poles, and, apparently, Russians. But what of the Jews? For some reason they are not mentioned. Thus far "in the territories of the Soviet Union" we have exterminated over 500,000 Jews and—as all three signers of the Declaration perfectly well know—we still have three or four hundred thousand more to go. Not to mention the fact that today in Auschwitz 9,326 South European Jews went to the ovens, and that approximately the same number went to them yesterday and will go to them tomorrow.

There's no mystery about it, no secret. Although we take care to see that it's never mentioned in the Reich and the occupied territories, today's world of double and triple intelligence agents makes it impossible to keep such massive operations secret from the enemy. Since no one in the world of intelligence is entirely faithful and no one is entirely treacherous, it follows that in general *we* know what the enemy knows, and that *he*, in general, knows what we know.

We know, for example, that their own intelligence services have informed Stalin and Churchill and Roosevelt exactly what our Jewish policy *is*, how it is *effectuated*, and (which is even more important) *where*. From this it follows that their Moscow Declaration is a signal to the world that large issues are not to be beclouded with gabble about the Jewish problem because in *this* game the Jews don't count.

17 August 1944

The last transport from Greece arrived today at Birkenau. They comprised the entire Jewish population of the island of Rhodes. Counting the dead, there were slightly over twelve hundred unbelievable poor and semi-literate peasants, traders, and petty usurers. I looked Rhodes up on my map. It is over two thousand miles from the borders of the Reich, which shows how far, even now, the Fuehrer's arm can reach. The consignees were transported from Rhodes to the Greek mainland by sea in caïques, and from there to Birkenau in sealed freight cars. This at a time when the Wehrmacht is preparing for the evacuation of the Greek archipelago; when partisans are openly raiding warehouses, supply dumps, and communication centers; and when, for lack of rail or motor transport, we are abandoning enormous stores of material. In other words, this last deportation train from Greece has taken precedence over the most pressing military necessities. Clearly the Fuehrer considers the Jew-cleansing of Europe to be of greater importance than victory itself.

There is a spiritual purpose here I've only lately begun to understand. Jew-free we can survive defeat itself and still, in some proper future time, achieve the victory that twice has been denied us; Jew-infested, no victory, now or in the future, can save us from the inevitable fate of peoples and nations who fail or refuse to excise the Jewish cancer from their guts.

The transport in question consisted of the poorest human material imaginable: eighty-six went to the work force, the rest to the showers.

21 August 1944

An ugly bit of carelessness with yesterday's contingent of Hungarians. A work squad sorting out clothing in one of the undressing sheds discovered a year-old child (female) crawling through the stuff, obviously hidden there and left behind by its mother. Guards were summoned, and the child was immediately shot.

Such incidents are always bad for the morale of custodial personnel, in this case particularly so because the child in question had blue eyes and the guard—Heintzel by name—whose duty it had been to kill her awakened in the middle of the night shouting that he'd murdered a German child and threatening to shoot anyone who came near him. Two men were killed and a third wounded before he was finally subdued and transferred to the psychiatric ward.

Stricter supervision of female undressing sheds has been ordered.

18 November 1944

I have feelings of exaltation. I love birds. Yesterday I gave cheese to a child. I am not one of the fatherless. I fish in meadows. I provide. I pretend. I premeditate. But not murder. I am a premeditator of goodness. Unrecognized goodness. Unrequited goodness. Unwanted goodness. Unneeded goodness. Unjustified goodness. Undesirable goodness. Extreme goodness, which is to say the goodness of God himself who gave life to man, beast, bird, and cockroach for the sole purpose of taking it away, of taking it back by stealth, by torment, bit by bit, cell by cell, until the cockroach dances itself to exhaustion, the bird sinks, the beast falls to his knees, and man, driven quite mad, drowns in the vomit of his own despair. To such a God I say, "You're a thief, a liar, a ravager, a holy barracuda, a sacred cannibal who feeds exclusively on the fruit of his own loins."

What's happening to me? I'm turning Jew. I'm talking to God. I'm *arguing* with him. I've watched them here, watched with bewildered astonishment those endless lines of shivering, grayheaded, knob-kneed old Jews shambling toward the gas chamber like mutilated insects, warmed by nothing more substantial than the stench of their own dung, and talking the whole distance, talking to God every step of the way, each in his own fashion, to be sure, but each sustained to the very end by the passion of that interminable colloquy with his maker.

There's a point to this. I'm not just babbling into my diary for the sake of literary exercise, I'm trying to extract one small kernel of sense out of the raging nonsense that fills my life. The kernel of sense is this: To debate with God is to bring him down (or to *try* to bring him down) to man's level, i.e., to the level of a human being who knows he must die. As such, it is an attempt on God's life, an act designed to complete itself in deicide. Having already killed God's son, the Jew's next move—indeed, his only logical move—has to be against the life of God himself.

Now even if there is no God, as mostly I'm sure there isn't, the *desire* to kill him (much less the actual attempt) is a crime. Beyond this, if you try to kill God, which any form of debate with him actually means, why be surprised if he retaliates by killing you? And that is the most remarkable thing of all about the Jew: he is *never* surprised by God's wrath, nor put off by his inconceivable thirst for Jewish blood. Since Jews are thus the only people who understand death and God's appetite for it, it follows that they're the ones who most deserve it if only because they're better prepared than the rest of us to receive it.

Thus we of the SS are actually engaged in God's work. Even more terrifying, we engage in it at the risk of becoming *like* God. The question is whether or not we dare take that risk: whether extermination of the Jew is actually worth risking admission to the terrible realm of Almighty God with all his avenging angels, his princes, his cherubim, and the forty-two frightful sanctities who surround his throne?

It seems clear to me that God is inhuman by any definition, and that so am I who faithfully does his work. Except—and there *are* exceptions in every case—except in certain weak and unmanly moments during which I listen to the crickets at night, to the dawn recognition call of infant birds, to the soft-rustling, deliberate courtship of snails on a leaf, to the shrill orgiastic murmurings of life that rage through the meanest weedpatch day after night after year to the end of time.

I'm saying Amen to you, God, Amen from Auschwitz where daily we do what your slightest gesture could have stopped us from doing had the doing of it not been thy will. I mumble prayers in my sleep—not for me but for you. Fuck you, God. Fuck you who has fucked every creature on earth from the beginning of time. Fuck you forever. Fuck you until I am as dead by your hand as thousands, tens of thousands, are already dead by mine. As one who knows you for what you are, and therefore no longer fears your terrible vengeance, I say fuck you forever, time without end, Amen.

26 November 1944

Orders came through yesterday and were announced today: liquidation of the Jews will cease immediately; gas chambers and crematoria will be dismantled as quickly as possible; hail Mary full of grace.

I observe with some interest that the order to kill no more came not from God nor his local delegate, the Pope, but from His Excellency, the Reichsfuehrer-SS Heinrich Himmler.

◆ 3 ◆

Grieben at Auschwitz

In the beginning of 1944 Grieben finds himself on a mission to the Eichmann office in Berlin. Walking with an SS comrade along the Unter den Linden, he spots a woman, a *young* woman, as he feels, no more than thirty-two, perhaps thirty-five years old; a smartly but not too expensively dressed woman whose brisk walk and confident bearing bespeak life at its flux, and a future to which she looks forward with something more than hope—a life she anticipates with *expectancy*. She is Liesel.

Through the good offices of SS friends he discovers her true identity. Although her maiden name, Dahlem, is legitimately German and therefore Aryan, her mother, born Levin, became Aryan only by marriage, which means that Liesel, under the Nuremberg Code, is a Jew. She is married to a physicist at the Max Planck Institute, whose name is honorably preceded by a *von*, and the mother of his two young children. Because of his scientific value to the state, her husband, through friends and perhaps a little bribery, has been able to secure for her a special dispensation which conceals all evidence of her half-Jewish origin.

The next day, while selecting children's stockings in a shop on the Friedrichstrasse, she is seized by SS agents. An hour later her clothing, stuffed into a paper bag and labeled with her name and number, is deposited by a reception clerk in the storage basement of SS Headquarters, Berlin, while Liesel, naked but for a towel and a small bar of medicated soap, stands before the allocation officer's small desk. She is assigned to Concentration Camp Auschwitz-Birkenau. Departure, 8:00 P.M. Special Transport. As she passes with her towel and soap toward the rear for medical examination and delousing procedures, she has no idea that Grieben's adoring eyes follow her from the other side of a one-way window disguised as a mirror. All that she sees reflected in its grime as she passes is despair.

At Auschwitz, two hours after passing through selection, Frau Liesel von Kordt is delivered in prison garb to the office of Sturmbannfuehrer Grieben, who indicates the day's admission list on his desk. He recognized her name and sent for her at once. He deplores the unhappy coincidence that after so many years has brought them together in circumstances so unfortunate. If he can be of any service. . . .

The instant she sees him Liesel knows precisely what has occurred, and why, and how she must deal with it. No friend or relative will ever be notified of what has happened to her or where she is, nor will inquiries from them ever be answered. All that will be known is that at a certain hour on a certain street in Berlin, some miracle of the law changed her from a human being to a statistic.

Once the fatal fact of her parentage came into SS hands, nothing could have prevented the next step and the next and so to the end. The only power that still remains to her is choice, the power to decide whether she will go to the ovens and certain death or to Grieben and a chance for life. She is still young, she has a husband whom she loves, two children who need her, and much to live for. She opts for Grieben in full understanding of the danger he represents: she knows the grossness of his spirit and the corruption which stands between his desire for love and his inability to give or accept it. She knows, in short, the risk she accepts in staking her love of life against Grieben's love of death.

She says, "I know why I'm here and I'll do anything to stay alive."

She is moved into a cubicle adjoining Grieben's office. Their struggle for survival continues for eighteen months as the war and the ovens of Auschwitz-Birkenau roar to a mutual climax. In a time when the Reich is besieged on two fronts by the massed armies of a dozen nations, at a moment when German survival depends on the swift transport of troops from east to west or west to east and south, entire divisions are immobilized for the passage (from Salonika and southern Greece to Auschwitz-Birkenau in Poland) of sixty trains, each consisting of fifty to a hundred cattle cars filled with human beings. The war has become holy—a war which, even though lost for Germany, will be won for mankind if Europe is cleansed of its last Jew before the curtain descends.

Here, then, is madness, the ultimate madness, the mating of science with Satanism, of politics with theology, of love with death, in a form and on a scale which Europe has never before known. Day and night long trainloads of human cargo rumble into the reception depot at Auschwitz. Day and night the inmate bands celebrate the rites of selection while the echoing gas chambers fill and empty and fill again and the ovens devour their predetermined quotas, blackening the sky by day, reddening it by night.

In such rituals no participant is sane, neither those who are to be killed nor those who are to kill them, for both are hopelessly engrossed in the death-infatuated ecstasy of love and hate, which always lies at the threshold of human dissolution. Despite the general apathy and despair which prevails in this vast compound of the doomed, there still remain those who hate death, who deny and defame and deride him. Among them arise strange cults for the celebration of sex, which is the origin of life, rather than death, which is its end. In the very shadow of the ovens by day, in the glow of their fires by night, men and women and sometimes even children come together in strange, unplanned saturnalias through which life and love are perceived purely as sex—pornographic sex, obscene sex, unnatural sex, wild, abandoned, and sometimes excremental sex—orgiastic affirmations of life in the shadow of that greatest of obscenities and perversions which is death himself, the ultimate enemy whom they mock and defile at the very moment his hand reaches for their throats.

Thus, also, with Grieben and the woman of his dreams—the first and only woman over whom he has absolute power, the woman whose living flesh must enact every fantasy that enters his mind, the woman whom he can clothe or unclothe as he wishes, whom he can openly fondle for the titillation of outsiders, whose favors he can offer to anyone he chooses while he stands with them as voyeur to observe the ways in which they are taken by the recipient and yielded by their involuntary donor. In the first month of their association Grieben's heightened sexuality causes him, quite inadvertently, to impregnate his wife with a third and unwanted child to bless their autumnal years.

Liesel, clinging fiercely to life, studies and obeys him as intently as a lion its trainer. She apprehends and measures every mood that rises and ebbs in the dark wastes of his hungering heart. When she perceives that his need calls for tears, she weeps; for humiliation, she abases herself; for entreaties, she begs; for punishment, she submits; for love, she drowns him in it. The only thing she denies him is the pleasure of overcoming her resistance, for she knows that in denying him this she denies him all—and denies it in a way he can't possibly resent, since what *manly* man can resent a woman's refusal to disobey even his most outrageous command?

The longer death moves hand in hand with his possession of Liesel, the wilder his infatuation becomes. When his wife births a baby girl he names the child Liesel so that he may utter the beloved name openly in his own house and freely adore it in the presence of his son, his daughter, his wife, and the Witnesses for Jehovah who are his servants. When the child dies three weeks later, he is inconsolable save for the comfort of Liesel's arms in the house of death, which has become their trysting place.

FROM TRUMBO'S NOTES

Once he gets her in Auschwitz, and once he has sent her to the brothel for the first day—he treats her with all the romanticism of first love; he tries, he asks, he begs, but he never forces—the result, as we discover, her underlying corruption.

This is the key. Her desolate corruption because *she* becomes the selector.

And they do, in the end, come together gently, lovingly, in their corruption.

When he gets her into Auschwitz, he *never* touches her—he *never* rapes her—he courts her. And what he cannot understand is that although he never uses force, still she does not love him. The greater his deference, the greater her resistance. Until, at last, they *almost* fall in love—with what the other is *not*.

◆

I think when he gets Liesel in Auschwitz he treats her with elaborate courtesy—gentleness, consideration, respect, genuine love. He enslaves himself to her.

Does she use him? Probably. This could be the form of his corruption. If she uses him to some certain lines—she herself has succumbed to the corruption—to the power of selection. It is this that destroys her morally and physically in the end. She *walked* to her death, invited it. The corruption is everywhere; it affects us all.

I think she, through him, has engendered an escape route.

Her problem—what right have I to save this child at the cost of an old man's life.

Does she have a diary—or a record intended for her husband—which he finds after her death and uses in his account (the novel) as if he had it at the time? Thus we get her posthumous account as a contemporary comment by her.

LIESEL'S DIARY

I too—

I too—am selecting my favorite Jew—and is it not—you, you, you! You who are only my husband by law—but never was—because I have found my lover—the only one who truly wants me and has beckoned to me always; his name is Death, and I have gone to him. Forever—and ever—and ever his. Death. Her diary. Write it, write it.

(He and I are the damned. We are engaged in a union and divine division that makes us one.)

Make it a true marriage between Grieben and Liesel—the only possible marriage open to either of them. In the midst of the world which is theirs. His last words are Liesel—Liesel—Liesel. . . . I shall come.

As 1944 draws to an end, the dream begins to fade. In the West the Allies move eastward through France; in the East the Russians are encamped on the Vistula. Such news filters down even to prisoners. In September, a special Sonderkommando prisoner rebels and manages to destroy Crematory IV. The uprising is drowned in blood and the killing resumes. Grieben's children join the youth services and leave home. He sends his wife to live with relatives in Dresden and abandons the most luxurious cottage he has ever lived in.

He moves into an apartment at SS Headquarters, Auschwitz, to live openly with Liesel. He clothes her in gowns and furs from Rome, Paris, Berlin, all confiscated when their owners, now deceased, first arrived at the camp. They dine on Westphalian ham, pâté from Strasbourg, caviar from the Volga, marzipan from Vienna, washed down with champagne and Rhine wine and Hungarian bull's blood.

In November, the SS Berlin orders the killings to be halted.

The camp is to be converted into a slave labor headquarters for the manufacture of arms and synthetic rubber. Early in December the gas chambers are blown up and the remaining crematoria destroyed on command of SS Headquarters Berlin. In that same month, only a week before Christmas, Grieben discovers that he is becoming impotent.

In January, 1945, the last German incursion into the Ardennes is repulsed, and the Western allies advance toward the sacred borderlands of the Reich itself. In the East the Russians open their last great offensive through Poland and, ultimately, Germany itself.

In Auschwitz-Birkenau the evacuation of able-bodied prisoners begins. Trains, trucks, even horse-drawn vehicles and marching columns move westward through winter snows for the distribution of prisoners to Bergen-Belsen and a dozen other camps, while SS personnel and Sonderkommandos labor frantically to destroy all evidence of what Auschwitz-Birkenau really was.

Through it all Liesel loyally supports and obeys her master, indulging whims and peculiar desires which daily become less tormenting, less degrading as Grieben's impotence increases and finally becomes absolute. He proposes to take her with him when complete evacuation is ordered. She gladly agrees. His emotional dependence upon her increases in direct proportion to the growing seriousness of his professional difficulties. The more his impotence prevents him from taking from her, the more his increasing passion for her expresses itself in odd, sometimes childlike, and often pathetic ways.

On the morning of January 17, 1945, the Russians enter Warsaw and the final evacuation of Auschwitz-Birkenau begins. The last Sonderkommando group is to be killed (as always), some 5,000 of the sick and infirm are to be left for the Russians, after which camp SS personnel will filter westward for new assignments.

Grieben orders Liesel to pack their bags while he goes to the village, takes his Skoda sedan (gift of a deceased Czech inmate) out of storage, and returns with it to the camp for Liesel and their belongings. It is three-thirty in the afternoon when he returns. Their bags are packed, but Liesel is not with them. She is not in his office. She is not in evacuation headquarters. He rushes from office to office, from department to department, until at last a guard informs him that an order went out to kill all Sonderkommandos and inmate office personnel before abandoning camp.

He rushes to the low brick building in which private mass executions are conducted. A work detail pulling a carrier loaded with bodies emerges from the building as Grieben enters it. There he finds her amidst a tangled heap of fresh-killed corpses. Habit is strong, prisoners' clothing is always sent to the warehouses, and SS efficiency, even in this emergency, has prevailed: Liesel and all her companions in death are nude.

Grieben lifts her from the floor, holds her in his arms. She has been shot through the left breast and again through the neck. She is still warm. Her brown hair, caught in the bend of his arm, streams down over one cheek and shoulder—as limp and lovely against the white of her skin as the seal-brown ears of a rabbit, a doe rabbit done to death by love on a summer lawn in the breathless silence of a time now three long decades dead.

He carries her to their quarters, washes her, dresses her, weeps for her. As twilight approaches he enfolds her in a blanket and places her in the rear seat of the Skoda, which was to have carried her alive from this place.

That night he buries her secretly in the forest. The next morning he joins in the general retreat.

Three days later, on the wintry road to Ratibor for Auschwitz personnel, among them Boekner, the officer who supervised the final action against Sonderkommandos and inmate office personnel. Boekner, who is a compassionate man by his own definition of compassion, explains to Grieben that he had no choice in the matter: Liesel's inclusion was mandatory by reason of the classification "inmate office personnel," which Grieben himself had assigned to her; the order had been given and he, Boekner, was bound by oath to obey it without exceptions of any kind, regardless of his own personal feelings. Grieben agrees; he has lived by that same code himself; he understands that the individual who executes an order cannot be blamed for the consequences of his obedience.

Greatly relieved that Grieben thinks no less of him for being a good soldier, Boekner tells him that as soon as the prisoners had undressed he ordered a subordinate to search for those small personal possessions which prisoners invariably secrete on their persons or in their clothing. He hands Grieben a small sealed packet, no larger than an ordinary-sized envelope, but slightly thicker. It was the least he could do, Boekner explains; surely a man deserves at least *some* memento no matter how small or inconsequential, to keep green the memory of one he has lost. . . .

When he is alone, Grieben opens the packet. It contains a needle, two buttons, four aspirin pills, a small length of narrow gauze bandage, a two-by-three-inch snapshot of a man with two children (a boy and a girl) climbing over him, and a sealed letter addressed to Herr Professor Doktor Heinrich von Kordt, Max Planck Institute, Berlin. Grieben opens the envelope. It contains a single sheet of his own SS stationery covered on both sides with Liesel's handwriting. It is dated January 17, 1945—the day of the evacuation. He remembers her excitement on that day, her gaiety, her eager plans for the new life opening up for them, her affection, her kisses.

"My dearest dearest Heinrich and my most darling of children . . ." She recounts her arrest, her arrival at Auschwitz, her assignment to "a man from whom I fled eleven years ago but who has caught me again and uses me as his whore—which oh my dear and my darling, I *am*." The Russians are everywhere; they are evacuating the camp; she will go with Grieben who has promised that she will no longer be an SS prisoner, but his mistress, "although he is now, thank God, much less than a man. I send this letter to let you know where I am. Soon I will write you again, so that you will be able to find me if you still want me. If you *do* want me—if you *truly* do—I pray that through love and forgiveness you will help to make me a human being again, even a woman. I have learned so much about love that I am trying to find a different word for it. Please find me. Please help me. Until you hold me once more in your arms, I am, whether in heaven or hell, forever your wife—Liesel."

So that's how it was. Lies, betrayal, corruption, filth. The infinite duplicity of woman. And yet I loved you, Liesel, I love you still, I loved you in life, I love you in death, I loved you in my earliest childhood, I will love you in the hour that I die, for without love there is nothing, without love there is only loneliness and despair and darkness—without love I am death himself.

Grieben's history from that moment forward is recounted in Chapter 1. Only small portions of it need be touched on as the novel ends. He has become an old man dreaming nightmares in the afternoon sun: he weeps again for the squirrel, for the doe rabbit, for Inge, for Morgen, for Winterfeld, for Blobel, and always, of course, for Liesel—the coarse, decadent dreams of nineteenth-century romanticism energized and made real by the twentieth century's vision of pragmatic materialism.

He sorrows for those he destroyed, yet he remembers and relives their agony with such loving re-creation of detail—even to the smallest moment of pain or humiliation—that it becomes clear the only reason he recalls them is to feel once more the pleasure they gave. Given the power, he would do it all over again in a welter of tears and rapture. He sorrows not for the loss of love, which he never understood or truly wanted, but for loss of the political power which enabled him to commit his crimes and of the sexual power which made them enjoyable.

But this, of course, he does not know. His perverted appetite for absolute power over an animal, a man, a woman, or over all animals, all men, all women, combined with the corruption of having actually possessed it, has blinded him to any suffering but his own, to any virtue except those he finds in his own life and personality. Commanded by voices from the dark forests of German pre-history (and *our* pre-history, perhaps?), he obeyed the call of the blood, the will of the German folk-soul, and the cry of old gods, treacherously slaughtered eons ago, yet still howling from the swamps for vengeance.

Almost suffocated with the melancholy of self-pity, with nostalgia for the glory and pain of all that has gone from the world, he embarks—an old man, lost, alone, the last bearer of a faith betrayed—on a pilgrimage to Auschwitz.

There, on a chill autumn day, he ascends a small rise that looks down on the deserted camp. He stares at the barracks, row on row; the abandoned headquarters buildings; the rubble which once loomed above the sky as gas chambers and crematoria, from which no smoke now rises; the desolation, the loneliness, the accursedness of a site which once provoked emotions never before known to men.

He remembers the sights and sounds of a hundred thousand human beings huddled together while six thousand of them went up in flames each twenty-four hours with fresh trainloads replaced every hour. He remembers the chimneys which belched black smoke and human souls into gray skies and low-hanging clouds.

He realizes that *any* place which witnessed the sacrifice of two million members of the human family in so short a time must by its very nature be a *holy* place; that the experience itself partook of holiness; and that he, Grieben-the-lost, was an attendant priest at those holy rites. Tears fill his eyes. He falls to his knees, lifts his arms toward the vast deserted temple in which his existence soared to its climax, and cries: "Israel, Israel, here in this holy place gave I unto thee thy soul. . . ."

AFTERNOTE

No synopsis is explicit. Characters change as they are written and take on lives of their own. The thing I am after here, the devil

I am trying to catch, is that dark yearning for power which lurks in all of us, the perversion of love which is the inevitable consequence of power, the exquisite pleasures of perversion when power becomes absolute, and the dread realization that in a time when science has become the servant of politics-as-theology, it can happen again. D.T.

Part III

THE GRIEBEN LETTERS

EDITOR'S NOTE

Trumbo wrote to his friend Angus Cameron, an editor at Knopf, giving his thoughts on Night of the Aurochs *and outlining the story. Across the top of his copy of the letter, Trumbo had scrawled: "I was in New York at the Algonquin Hotel." The first two chapters of the novel, delivered the same day, April 17, 1961, were included. An earlier draft, dated November 28, 1960, was probably the first writing Trumbo had done on the project. Except for the eighteenth-century-style headnotes, the text of the April 17, 1961, version is identical with the one in this book.*

April 17, 1961

Dear Angus,

About the novel. I think I want to call it "Night of the Aurochs." Authorities differ as to whether the aurochs was a primitive European bison from which European cattle descended, or whether it was itself a primitive cow. They also seem unclear as to whether there are any aurochs presently existing. But these are small matters beside the fact that Goering had beasts which he swore were aurochs at Karinhall, lavished great care on them, and shot them with considerable ceremony. The zoological primitivity of the aurochs struck me as rather an apt corollary to the political primitives who called themselves Nazis. There is something dark and recessive in both. Of course readers won't know what an aurochs is, but that doesn't seem very important to me. I doubt they knew what a Babbit was until they read the book.

I intend to use a variety of styles and methods as the book gets under way: first person present tense, first person past, excerpts from diaries, etc., with, I hasten to assure you, sections comprised almost entirely of dialogue.

In the fourth chapter, Grieben, at the age of seventeen and in the last months of World War I, joins the Bavarian army, sees action, and makes three friends. The first is blinded in battle; the second becomes a male homosexual prostitute in Berlin of the early 1920s; the third joins the SA with Grieben about 1929. Grieben shifts to the SS in 1933, and in 1934—"The Night of the Long Knives"—liquidates his SA comrade who failed to make the organizational jump in time.

When the war is lost, the three friends join the Freikorps mainly because there is nothing else for them to do, and enthusiastically put down Poles and Russians in the east, Communists in Berlin and Spartacists in Bavaria. In Munich, Grieben for the first time hears Hitler—in the very early days of the early twenties—and I hope to reproduce the emotional atmosphere of the times and the leader.

Grieben ends in Berlin from about 1925 on. That city, in the throes of depression, inflation and *free choice* (which was the greatest moral crisis for the obedient, well-organized German) becomes the real background for his following development. It is here he meets, courts, and marries a girl two years older than he, not because he loves her, but because she has a small house free and clear—such rare security in those times that, although unbeautiful, she is greatly sought after. She presents him with two children in quick succession—children he doesn't very much want.

He spends most of his time in the easy communal barracks of the SA, where there is the security of numbers, of a purpose, plus a place to sleep, and a way to eat. The appeal of this life to the rootless and disorganized German youth is fairly clear. It was rather jolly—and one always had Jews, Communists, and Social Democrats to bully, which gave a pleasant sense of power and program.

About 1932, in Berlin Grieben falls in love with a young dancer (café) and courts her furiously. She is attracted to him, but at the same time afraid of him. He begs her to be his mistress; she refuses. He begs his wife for a divorce; she refuses. This is the first time Grieben has experienced passionate romantic love, and it almost drives him insane.

On the night of the burning of the books, amid banners and chants and songs and bands and torches, he takes her to a park within sight and sound of the book-burning frenzy, and rapes her. However, he ejaculates prematurely and thus merely soils her. He is overcome with embarrassment, but attributes the mishap to his excess of virility. He never consummates the affair with the girl. The next morning she has vanished, and not until years later does he see her.

He passes through the "Night of the Long Knives," executes his last friend, and goes off to SS training school. Here the intellectual doctrine of anti-Semitism is pounded into his head as pure German classicism (which it may be), dating from Luther, and reflected regularly in every generation by the most revered intellectuals and artists of the German people. Here I hope to show from all classical sources of German education that anti-Semitism as a doctrine has been drilled endlessly into the minds of German youth, until it became an article of faith, and had been so for a hundred years. The Nazis didn't invent the article, they merely invoked it, and carried it through with absolute German logic.

Then his slow rise—Dachau, Bergen-Belsen, Buchenwald, and finally, on the third level of command, Auschwitz-Birkenau. There he lives with his wife and teen-age children (both of whom leave home before the war is over for national service), in a lovely cottage, staffed by Jehovah's Witnesses from the camp, with flower gardens fertilized by materials he brings from the camp, whose great smokestacks constantly becloud the sky above his house. By day he fulfills his duties of extermination.

In the course of 1944, he finds himelf on a mission to the Eichmann office in Berlin. Walking along the street one day with an SS comrade, he spots a young woman across the street—it is the girl, the dancer, the loved one.

Through the good offices of friends on SS security, he has her traced, discovers her true identity. Although her maiden name was German, he discovers that her mother was Jewish—and understands somewhat better her reticence to have a liaison with him.

She is married to a physicist of good German family—a von—who works at the Max Planck Institute. She has two young children. By special dispensation, and a little connivery, her husband has managed to conceal all evidence of her half-Jewish origin. But once Grieben is on the trail, she is lost. Three days later she is picked up off the street by the SS, and seen no more by her husband, family or friends.

As a favor to Grieben she is transported in a special van to Auschwitz. He places her in a special room in camp headquarters, immediately adjoining his office, and there enjoys her favors—all possible favors—while insisting that he loves her. As a matter of fact, he does love her in the only way he can conceive of love—the area in which love is related to sadism and death.

In this eighteen-month period of his life, while the extermination camps roared to their climax (together with his affair with his slave), I wish to investigate the whole curious phenomenon of sex-as-death which seemed to dominate Auschwitz at that time, even among certain groups of prisoners, who held their own saturnalias of sex in the very shadow of the ovens.

His heightened sensibilities cause him, unexpectedly and unwillingly, to fertilize his wife, who presents him with an autumnal daughter. He names the child after his slave in the camp, so that he may openly speak the adored name in front of his wife without arousing suspicion or unpleasantness.

Then comes the Russian advance. The slow realization the camp must be abandoned. He sends his wife and daughter rearward. He and others labor like dogs in the final exertion of extermination. The kapos revolt, an oven is blown up, and the main body of prisoners begin their terrible march toward the German heartland. On the last day in camp, all preparations being made, Grieben goes to headquarters to get his slave. She isn't in her quarters next to his office. He demands to know what happened, is told somebody gave out the order that all inmate personnel were to go to the gas chambers and the ovens.

Howling with rage and anguish, he goes to the gas chamber. Their last service has just been performed. He goes to the ovens, and there amid the corpses, he finds the body of his beloved, still warm. He pulls his gun, kills three kapos who are engaged in cutting her hair and preparing her for incineration. He picks her up in his arms, weeping. Her brown hair streams backward against her white body. She is his rabbit, once again his murdered love. He buries her secretly in the forest and joins in the general retreat.

From this point the opening chapter carries it forward—his loss of family, his return to Forchheim, his prison sentence, and his lonely cottage. Having lived through the experience of his life, he is, at the end of the book, impelled by the enormity of his experiences and of his loneliness, to return to Auschwitz, a one-man pilgrimage toward his beginnings.

On a little rise that gives a view of the camp, he stares at the rows of barracks, the abandoned headquarters, the ovens from which no smoke rises, the swampy surroundings, the drifting mist, the desolation, the loneliness of a site which once provoked emotions (as he feels) never before known to man. He remembers the sights and sounds of a hundred thousand persons huddled together, while twenty thousand of them went up in flames every twenty-four hours, and fresh trainloads replaced them. He remembers those chimneys when they belched forth great clouds of smoke. He feels that *any* place which beheld two million murders in so short a while must be a holy place; that the experience in itself partook of holiness; and that he himself was, in a sense, a priest at holy rites. He falls to his knees, lifts his arms toward the vast sacrificial altar, and says (in effect)—"Israel, Israel, here I gave thee thy soul!"

I should, as you know, have to place a thousand qualifications on every phrase written above, but to do that, it will be necessary to write the book.

All the best,

DALTON

EDITOR'S NOTE

This undated letter from Michael Wilson, screenwriter and close friend of Trumbo, was probably written in late 1973 or 1974. Trumbo had sent him the first eight chapters. (He had an earlier version of the first four, which could not be located in Trumbo's papers on the novel and may possibly have been the same version Wilson had read in Rome ten years before.)

Tuesday

Dear Old Boy:

I received your manuscript last Saturday and have been reading it with vast appreciation at every spare moment I could find since then. I am even more impressed with these eight chapters than I was with the four I read in Rome ten years ago.

I wish some way could be found to prevent you from taking on more film work until you have finished the novel. It would be folly to rely on your own character for this essential discipline, because the mere jingling of coins triggers a conditioned reflex in your arthritic write [sic] hand. If your loving wife and younger daughter were made of sterner stuff, they could intercept calls from agents and producers and turn them away. Alas, they have the frailty of their sex and want you to be happy—and you are happy only when making lots of money. But I know—and perhaps even you now suspect—that Heaven did not give you your recent reprieve and let you remain in this vale of tears in order to be happy, but to finish this novel.

I have a compromise solution. The Lenten season is fast approaching. Why don't you give up screenwriting for Lent? As I once, at the age of ten, gave up the reading of funny papers? This sacrifice would give you six weeks on the book, and only God knows how many words you can write in six *uninterrupted* weeks.

My one negative observation on the first eight chapters has to do with the material about Inge. I have a hunch it is overlong in the total context of the novel. (This may be a foolish comment because I don't really know the total context.) More important, a portion of the material about Inge strikes the only false note I find in the manuscript. Your celebration of the pubescent (or prepubescent) female form is pure Trumbo (which by definition means that it is very good writing indeed) but it is not Grieben. The prose here is both lyrical and comedic, and if I understand Grieben he is incapable of combining these two qualities in one vision.

Wednesday

I have finished reading the entries from the diary. This is powerful stuff. I have a few questions about the diary—and I do mean questions, not criticisms. I'm not sure I understand its function within the body of the memoir. To begin with, the keeping of a diary would certainly be forbidden to anyone engaged in mass extermination. How do you propose to get around this fact? You see, Grieben would have have been violating his oath and endangering his military career by keeping such a diary. Yet he decides to do so, to record the unspeakable for some possible future use. Therefore his very act becomes a kind of protest against the horrors he commits; it casts a shadow of doubt on the extermination policy itself. But that is not all. The diary is an anguished testament—wittingly or unwittingly, a confession of human misgivings. While Grieben might never admit to guilt or remorse, his nervous breakdown itself is a revelation that his soul is not yet dead and cries out against the atrocities the body must commit.

How do you reconcile the diarist of 1945 with the memoirist of 1973? The old man is full of certitudes as an unregenerate and unrepentant Nazi. Would he not reject the man who wrote that diary as weak and vacillating? Would he not, indeed, destroy the diary, and retell the events of 1945 as seen from the lofty perspective of 1973?

I am not suggesting that the diary be removed from the book. But since the elder Grieben is armored with self-justification, you and he must find a reason to justify its being there.

I'll send this letter along now and, with your permission, keep the manuscript a few days longer so I can reread certain portions.

Love to you and all your clan,

MIKE

EDITOR'S NOTE

Wilson's letter touched a sensitive spot: Trumbo's habit of letting the novel dangle if screenplay offers were available. It also triggered the remarkable letter below in which Trumbo blames "that particularly malignant form of mysticism called morality" for the holocaust, and seems to explain the role of Nazis like Grieben as instruments of some larger and mysterious purpose. Trumbo wrote across the top of his copy of the letter, "Sometime in 1974."

Dear Lad,

Thanks for your letter and thanks particularly for the questions you raised about (a) the Inge woman, and (b) the diaries. They are exactly the sort of thing I need, and very often. When I comment on both subjects here, I do so not to challenge what you said but to clarify my thoughts about them—and the only way I will ever be able to clarify a thought is to put the goddamn thing on paper. It is also easier to write to you about such thoughts than to write about them to myself.

Your points about the Inge chapters are (a) that they are "lyrical and comedic" in a way the Grieben I have created can't possibly be; and (b) that they are overlong.

I completely agree with (a). The problem here is that Grieben, as presented, was written about ten years ago and the Inge stuff was in the last three years, and that possibly as I move ahead my concept of Grieben is changing somewhat from that of the man I started with so long ago. By the time I have finished the novel, if ever, it now seems quite clear to me that I shall have to go back and change the Grieben who opens the novel to match the Grieben he will have to become at the end. There are a good many reasons why I will have to do this in any event: he will have to be older (born in 1898) to participate in World War I, as I want him to, and his rise in the Party, SA and SS ranks will have to be considerably different than I made them in the first and second chapters. Not only this, but his *experiences* seem to be turning out to be somewhat different from the experiences I predicted for the Grieben I originally intended. I cannot make him a person who could recall Inge in terms of both lyrical and comedic (comedic in the sense of a mature man recalling the gaucheries of his boyhood). I will simply have to cut such passages, or change them to conform to his character. However, I feel I *need* this lyricism because so much of his life is concerned with problems of sexual love.

(I wonder here if, in dwelling on Inge as lyrically, as comedically as I have, I have not sunk to the level of pornography? If that which is lyrical is not made so in order to titillate the reader sexually? If that appears to the reader to be his intent, then it is pornographic, no matter how I try to defend it. I would like to hear your thoughts about this.)

Point (b) on overlength may also be true. I dwelt on Inge and the Inge business so long and in such detail because it presages other sexual events to come—events which establish the cultural and sexual obsessions which cause Grieben to *abuse* women in the guise of loving them. He is incapable of genuine sexual love. When I say *cultural* as well as sexual obsession, I mean that aspect of Teutonic culture which seems always to have drawn German *males* together in great marching herds, to almost complete exclusion, separation, and segregation of women. It was, in a sense, the passive homosexuality of the locker room, rather than the active homosexuality of the closet or the drag hall.

But it is not really a question of homosexuality; it is a question of the male herd in the development of the German nation. The male herd as tribal warriors. The male herd against the invading legions of Rome. Here, in my view, occurred one of the great disasters in German, or Teutonic, history: the male herd, the Germanic tribes, halted Rome's advance with the result that Roman civilization did not for centuries penetrate beyond the Rhine. Thus, the benefits of Roman law, Roman technology, and later of Christianity, were for centuries denied the German people, nation, community, tribe, or whatever you wish to call it.

Whether the civilizing influence of Rome was good or bad is quite beside the point that it became the dominant factor in the development of the rest of Europe, and that the Roman-civilized portion of Europe became the dominant force in the development of the entire continent. The Germans thus came to it late, which meant that as England, France, Holland, Sweden, Denmark, Spain and even Russia became *nations* the Germans still remained, in effect, a group of tribes, each tribe defended by its separate male herd, rather than the amalgamation of tribes (a nation) defended by a professional army.

Thus for two centuries, the principalities, kingdoms, duchies, and electorate of the German tribes had been little more than highways for the conquest and passage for foreign armies—French, Italian, Dutch, Swedish, Russian, etc., etc. When not prostrate beneath invading armies of one European power or another, the fragmented German states, manipulated from within and without, engaged in terrible social and religious wars against each other—wars which were always exploited by those European powers which had become what the Germans had not—i.e. nations. During the Thirty Years' War, the stature of German adults diminished by one inch!

The truth is that the German tribes, dominated by their male herds, never truly accepted Roman law, or Christianity, or Western philosophy or, after Napoleon, the concept of the Enlightenment, revolution, and libertarian democracy. Indeed, having suffered so much at the hands of those who accepted or inherited such concepts, why *should* they have felt impelled to accept them?

What *did* take root amid these centuries of misery was a terrible and quite understandable longing for nationship (which they didn't get until 1870, and then imperfectly). A nation could not come into being without leadership, hence their terrible longing for, need of, and dependence on, a leader. In order for the leader to preserve the nation he needed authority. The absolute authority of the absolute leader of the absolute State supported by the authority of the male herd, hence of the male. Male authority in the State, the church, the school, the home.

The absolutism of male authority is what Bismarck gave them, and later Wilhelm II. When it collapses at the end of World War I, it did not blame its collapse on its absolutism but on its "corruption" by Western liberalism which is riddled with Social Democracy (Marxist and Jewish), and city-oriented (feminine and Jewish) rather than nature-oriented (masculine and Aryan-Teutonic). Thus, the apocalyptic male absolutism of the Nazi which, aside from its political and territorial ends, resulted in the total subjugation of woman, and extermination of the Jews.

German history in populist literature is filled with examples of German desire to be *loved* by the world—a desire constantly frustrated by the not uniquely Teutonic conviction that the only true love is that which follows total subjugation. Just so with the man

Grieben. His whole personal life is a yearning for a woman's sexual love, a yearning that is never fulfilled, because love to him is conquest, subjugation, and abuse of the beloved. Thus,

1) what could have been a rather pleasant pubescent adventure for both him and Inge degenerated into attempted subjugation and fantasies of genuine abuse.

2) the next woman in his life, Beata, he married only because she owned a cottage free and clear during the inflation. Although with her he has two children and ultimately at Auschwitz a third, his rare sexual interludes with her are quick and brutal, and his abuse of her takes the form of complete sexual neglect.

3) the only woman he truly loves, almost to the point of distraction and insanity, is a member of the corps de ballet of the Berlin Opera. Because of his SS uniform she is afraid of him, hence goes out with him, but really resists seduction and even refuses his offer to divorce his wife and marry her. On the night of the great book bonfire in the square in front of the Berlin University, he takes her to a park across from the University square, and there rapes her, except for the fact that he ejaculates a quarter second before entry—ejaculates and soils her. In the midst of his anguished apologies for what he calls an excess of masculine sexuality, she vanishes into the darkness.

4) From that moment forward her disappearance is complete. She never returns to the opera; she never returns to her apartment; she simply ceases to exist. All Grieben and his comrades can discover about her is that she has *one* Jewish grandparent.

5) Years later, when Grieben, a major at Auschwitz, visits Berlin, he spots her on the street and puts an SS check on her. She is the wife of a professor at the Max Planck Institute and the mother of two young children.

6) Without knowing that Grieben has had anything to do with it, the young woman (Liesel) is picked up and sent to Auschwitz. There Grieben comes across her, "rescues her," has her assigned to his personal service. There, with total power over her person (and "loving" her to the point of madness) he does every sexual

thing to her in fact and life that actually he only fantasized doing with Inge. The pornographic fantasy of the child becomes a terrible reality of the man. What was completely innocent in Grieben the boy turns Grieben the man into a killer—not only a mass killer of the detested Jew, but the personal killer of the only woman he ever loved. Liesel dies, not at his hands, but in the general confusion evacuating Auschwitz in the face of the Russian advance.

7) While in Fulgenberg Prison, Grieben reads the first German translation of Anne Frank's diary and denounces it in his diary as a forgery, a plot of the Jews. However, 900,000 copies of the diary are printed in Germany alone and in its wake some books which confirm not only the validity of the diary, but reveal that Anne Frank and her family arrived at Auschwitz in September 1944.

8) Knowing now that the diary is undoubtedly valid and that Anne was actually an inmate at Auschwitz (transported to Bergen-Belsen when the Russians drew close), he begins to believe that he *knew* this 15-year-old child at Auschwitz, and that while she was there he *helped* her, and that in the course of helping her she began to *love* him. And he her.

9) When he is released from jail in 1953 (after six years) the first thing he does after settling in his tiny house in Forchheim, is to sell a few small possessions in order to go to Amsterdam, where the hiding rooms of the Franks had become a war memorial open to the public.

10) He arrives in Amsterdam, a man of 56, pays the admission fee, and wanders through the rooms remembering every incident in the life of the girl who celebrated her 15th birthday there. He sees the room in which she slept, the downstairs cubicle in which she and her sister bathed (and almost sees the bathing there); the attic window from which Anne and Peter looked down on the nightscape of Amsterdam below; the room in which she and Peter spoke "quite frankly" about menstruation—and the spot on which she kissed Peter on the mouth for the first time.

11) That night he wanders to the canal at the rear of the Franks' warehouse, and sits down on its bank, stares at the blind windows of Anne's hiding place. And then, quite suddenly, she appears beside him—a young woman of 24. She thanks him gently for all the kindness he did her at Auschwitz, when he begs her forgiveness for what his duty as a soldier compelled him (as others) to do to her—i.e. to kill her—she forgives him completely.

12) For years thereafter in Forchheim she comes to him at night as a sexual fantasy of *perfect* sex. She becomes the only woman in his life who ever truly loved him. She becomes his salvation, his consolation, his life. When he is 60 she comes to him as a woman of 29. When he is 65 she comes to him as a woman of 34, always loving him, always forgiving him, and then when he is 68 and his beloved Anne is 37—the age at which Liesel died in Auschwitz—she dies in his bed. He buries her in the woods outside Forchheim near the point where he killed the squirrel while a boy, just as he buried Liesel in the woods outside Auschwitz.

It is the death of his spectral and beloved Anne Frank which sends him, in his 70th year, on a pilgrimage to Auschwitz. The book ends as he looks down this horrid landscape, sees the chimneys belching forth their smoke, envisions once more the death of Liesel, the lovely presence of Anne Frank, sinks to his knees and cries out, "Remember, remember me Israel, for here in this holy place gave I unto thee thy soul!"

What I am after here, without being able to state it very clearly, is the sexual, political, and mystical fuck up which seems to me to be inherent in the history of the German people, and particularly in the Nazi period. The immolation of six million Jews was a God-like act. It is true that between five and six million non-Jews also met death in the extermination camps, just as it is true that perhaps fifty millions died in the course of the entire war. But the death of those six million Jews was unique, unprecedented, a completely new event in man's history. It was so far beyond war and peace and human nature and natural evil as to become a spiritual event, a mystical event, a true "act of God" which is to say the ultimate madness, the final insanity, the apocalypse.

Anyhow, that is the direction my thoughts have taken.

About the diary. There are no more confirmed diarists than the Germans. The more hideous their crimes, the more detailed the records they make of them. It is my intention to have Grieben, on the advice of his father, begin to keep a diary when he volunteers at the age of 17 for service in W.W. I. I think I can find believable reasons why, despite military regulations and oaths, he continues to keep his diary from W.W. I to the end of his life. Most of the photographs we have of atrocities—both in the occupied territories and in their camps—were taken by German soldiers in flagrant disobedience of orders. Letters and diaries, against all odds, further enrich the record. Throughout two horrible wars the German soldier marched into battle with the absolute conviction that he was, individually and as a group, writing a glorious new chapter in the history of the world, and he wanted to keep a record of his contribution to that history and that glory. (Let me kill the generalization here by saying that Grieben wanted to keep such a record.)

The reason that I, his biographer, need his diary to refer to from time to time throughout the last three quarters of the book, is that a diary records the emotion of an event at the time it occurred—a diary is the present time—whereas the narrative method of his autobiography tells only what he remembers of an event twenty or thirty years later. I desperately need both modes, both methods of narration.

In the opening chapter I intend to have him stare at two cardboard cartons held together by ropes, and to realize that those two shabby cartons contain the whole history of his life. He could die tomorrow, and it would really make no difference, his actual life would remain behind from birth certificate to the pension receipt he signed yesterday. The boxes where some men leave monuments, buildings, highways, palaces, histories. Two shabby boxes represent all that needs to be known, or will ever be known, about his life. Unless, of course, he clarifies the record by the book he is now beginning to write: the final cry of justification, necessarily of self-pity, the latter being one of the constant factors in *popular* German philosophy, history, memorials, and autobiography.

Members of the SA and the SS—all volunteers, all probably fanatics, all opportunists—nonetheless were called upon (even compelled) to commit acts and carry out operations which would have been unthinkable to the regular combat forces of the Wehrmacht, or regular army. Indeed, the army was *protected* from the necessity of committing such atrocities and, insofar as possible, was kept in relative ignorance of them. But those swaggering bullies who survived the purge of the SA and those who comprised the vast forces of the SS were called upon hourly and daily and always to commit crimes against humanity which the most diseased and opportunistic conscience cannot tolerate or carry through without suffering hideous psychic damage. Although individuals here and there are quite comfortable in the commission of monstrous crimes, it seems to be quite true that, as a generality, there is a limit to the evil man can bring to pass without destroying himself.

Thus it occurred that a major problem of those in high echelons of the SA, and particularly the SS, was the maintenance of anything resembling morale among the hundreds of thousands in the lower ranks who carried through the tortures and did the actual killing. The worst brutes and the most fanatical killers consumed enormous amounts of spirits, drugs, women, or whatever else was on hand to dull the anguish and malaise that were slowly robbing them of their humanity. They felt ill, they ran beserk, they went mad—apparently in large numbers—without once losing faith in their cause, without the slightest understanding of what it was that was driving them mad; without, in fact, knowing that they *were* mad or being driven so.

The leaders knew what was happening to them and reinforced their disease-ridden symptoms with special privileges, special dispensations, special philosophical reassurances, rewarding advances in rank, and promises of great honors and awards to come when the hopeless battle was won. Curiously enough, in all its operations, there were two crimes in the SS which carried severe punishment at the very end: (a) individual and unauthorized acts of sadism, and (b) theft. How crazy can a system be or become? Apparently there is no limit. Good Nazis spent every hour of their lives from 1925 to 1933 pursuing a holy fantasy and from 1933 to 1945 making of that fantasy an historical truth. Thus, when I deal with Grieben, I am dealing with a madman.

I wish to present him, to the very end of his life, as a convinced and even a fanatical Nazi, who nonetheless was fatally wounded by the atrocities he was obliged to commit which violated his humanity, yet were carried through manfully and resolutely in the course of duty to a holy cause. Abraham was prepared to kill Isaac, his son, in fulfillment of his duty to, and his love of, God. Also, blessed sacrifice has always been the test of man's devotion to a holy cause. Grieben did his job and suffered his punishment for a cause he believed encompassed the salvation of mankind. In doing the job he destroyed his spirit, he spoiled his life, and violated the essence, the spirit, the conscience, the very soul of a young boy who once grieved for a squirrel he brutally shot, and wept for an infant rabbit he had tortured to death. And despite all his grief, all the anguish and revulsion he feels for a lifetime's horrible crimes, he committed them for a high purpose, a shining cause. He was, therefore, by definition a hero. Even a moral hero if one wishes to put the matter in those terms. True he was a hero of a Satanic rather than a godly morality, but nonetheless the hero of a morality which after all was a morality of the *spirit*.

I am convinced that it is only in the context of mysticism—false mysticism, if you wish (but does that not imply the existence of a true mysticism?)—that the holocaust can be explained. Economics doesn't explain it, politics doesn't explain it, history doesn't explain it, sociology doesn't explain it, psychiatry doesn't explain it, Hannah Arendt's banality of evil doesn't explain it, nothing but mysticism can explain it and, specifically, that particularly malignant form of mysticism called morality. Since no person is uncertain in his own mind about what morality *is*, what it *means*, or that it is *good*, it follows there can be no doubt or uncertainty about the wisdom [a line is dropped in the letter] the rest of the world; and that in the cause of such imposition, such replacement of evil with good, no *necessary* act, however violent (Hiroshima) or cruel (Auschwitz), can be ruled out by truly believing moral men.

Do you see how suspicious I have become in my autumnal years of the very idea of morality as a fact or a cause? A great many Nazis remained, even in defeat, convinced of the righteousness, morality, of their ends, yet emerged (many of them) from the ordeal tormented and psychically wounded by memories of the means they had used to achieve their ends. There was also a measure of disappointed opportunism in their regrets. They had set out to conquer the world, to impose upon it a new order which would endure for a thousand years. When the great moral crusade ended in unconditional surrender, what had they gained from a lifetime struggle and a generation's blood?—the death of six million defenseless Jews! And it was precisely for this small end (world conquest would have been *so* much better) that they committed their most terrible atrocities, befouled themselves and their country, and lost their souls.

The memory of the holocaust is still so terrible to those who had a hand in it that most of them swear that they didn't know anything about it, or if they knew about it they opposed it, or that if they participated in it they were compelled to do so against their will. They make these assertions not only as a legal defense while on trial, but in memoirs written long after they had paid the price for their crimes. The thing is simply too horrible to be admitted. Julius Streicher's tears when he was shown photographs of tortured Jews at Nuremberg were nonetheless real tears, despite the fact that to the very end he was a real Nazi. Just so, Rudolf Hoess, Commandant of Auschwitz, asserting at his trial that the public would have never understood of the Commandant of Auschwitz that "he too had a heart and that he was not evil."

Anyhow, so it goes, and so do I blunder toward the heart of this goddamned book I should never have started. And because of Johnny. And the enormous (for me) sums I lost on it, and the hundred thousand dollars I still owe, partly to [name deleted] which financed it under Harry Margolis (and holds in trust everything we own—*everything*) and partly to the law firm of Margolis, MacTerman, etc., I am driven by sheer economic necessity to scramble (at the age of 68) for every movie dollar that passes my door. Since the offers still come in (for reasons I can't explain) that alone represents a triumph of age over obsolescence which ordinarily would give me a certain sense of satisfaction.

At the moment, as you know, I am finishing a script for the [. . .] Scarlatti inheritors. Four to six more weeks should do it. However, no matter what I am working on, not a week passes that I don't get *something* written on *Aurochs* or *Grieben*, or whatever the hell it will end up being called. Provided I can make certain minimal arrangements when I finish the *Scarlatti*, I intend to take at least four to six months from everything and finish the book.

As to health, everything seems okay as it can be for an idiot my age. My squadron of quacks at last have worked out the proper digitalis balance. Now that *that's* done—and it took them four months to do it!—the heart is no problem. The right lung keeps on doing the work of two as well as can be expected. I don't lift heavy things or take long walks or run after lost opportunities anymore, but I can still put in a good 9 to 5 day, and the quacks, ten months after the event, find no suspicion of recurrence of the cancer which convinces them they got it all. If so, fine; if not, fuck it. Incidentally, your letter stirred my mind to some rather active thinking for which I am extremely grateful.

Love to all the Wilsons

DALTON

EDITOR'S NOTE

Trumbo wrote his agent Shirley Burke the following undated letter enclosing some rewrites from the novel. It was undoubtedly written a few months before his death on September 10, 1976. Some material, where indicated, relating to contract negotiations, has been left out. He explains the parallels between his own life and Grieben's, speaks with amazing detachment about the fatal condition he has decided to incorporate into the characterization of Grieben.

Dear Shirley,

I am enclosing a few re-writes from a novel which will probably undergo a considerable sea-change before it is finished. This is my first uninterrupted prose work in years and I am enjoying it immensely. I will, of course, enjoy it much more if it turns out to be any good.

What I am sending you begins with a chapter five that didn't exist earlier and ends in the middle of a new chapter ten. What I am trying to do is trace the pattern of human cruelty from early childhood to the slobbering senility of old age. I am not trying to trace a consistent pattern because I don't think there is one. The pattern changes with individual growth and circumstances.

Insofar as my personal knowledge and even memory goes, all children are cruel, a few of them unwittingly, but most of them not. There may be an occasional saintly exception, but I doubt it. Very few of them are cruel all of the time, and all but a few of them are kindly part of the time, but cruelty is always there. They are cruel to creatures weaker than they, to creatures stronger if they dare; to those who love them and those who hate them—they are often especially cruel to each other.

I am sure there are almost as many scientific explanations of cruelty as forms of it; but I suspect that the simplest explanation lies in the fact that cruelty is fun; that it gives pleasure, and that the pleasure it gives is like no other because it is not really pleasure, but that most delightful masquerade for pleasure which is debauchery.

As we grow older our natural pleasure in cruelty yields to the pleasure of society, the cultural influences which surround us, and perhaps, more than anything else, to the urgent need for love and its rewards. Result: an organized society and a civilized world. Occasionally, however, the cruelty which is dormant in all of us breaks forth along the Somme, in Verdun, Stalingrad, Dresden, Hiroshima—and Auschwitz.

That is why I have devoted so much space to my protagonist's almost banal childhood cruelties. Unhappily, the social pressures and cultural influences which shaped him from, say, 1910 through 1923, far from diminishing his natural pleasure in cruelty exalted it to a virtue, made it the cornerstone of a new and brutal ideology, and used it as a weapon for the murder of millions.

With that explanation, or apology, or whatever else one might call it, I will move forward to the publishing contract which I have just given a careful reading:

[Several pages dealing with contract negotiations are left out.]

One thing I have forgotten to mention: a new element has entered the novel about which I have said nothing, either to you or to Marc. Originally, Grieben was my age (born in 1905)—an old man trying to tell a story of his life, or at least explain its failures. However, in order to get him into World War I, I had to make him older than I. Born now in 1898, he is probably 77 or 78 when he begins to tell his story.

Now here is where life sometimes comes to the assistance of fiction (I refuse to use the word "art") and the author's good or bad fortune adds not only to the drama of his fiction, but to his personal knowledge of what he is writing about. As you know, I had my left lung removed for cancer in 1973 at the age of 68, and three days later suffered what was misdiagnosed as a coronary infarction, but was really the onset of an irreversible but often controllable heart disease called chronic corpulmonale.

At a certain point in the novel it will become known that this is exactly what happened to Grieben at the age of 73 or 74—a pneumectomy plus chronic corpulmonale. He survives them, just as I have survived them for the last three years. (With any luck it is not unreasonable of me now to hope for another two or three years—as could be true with Grieben, despite the fact that he is somewhat my senior.)

Knowing that his life is almost at an end, he finds himself seized with a passion to record it on paper, to clarify the record, to leave behind him at least one bit of evidence to prove that once he existed on this earth and played at least a small part in its affairs. Medically, there are two reasons why the chances are fair that he will live long enough to finish the project: a) although after three years he is not completely safe from cancer, the disease gives fair warning of its presence, and death from it would come slowly enough to give him time to finish his job with the aid of pain-killers; and, b) chronic corpulmonale is not one of those dramatic affairs which kill swiftly and without warning. Death comes much more slowly—a steady weakening of the heart's ability to perform its job until it simply wears out, becomes too congested to function, yields to a siege of pneumonia or any other convenient disease. There is really nothing to it at all in the nature of *surprise*.

Grieben, in short, is engaged in a life and death struggle to finish the story of his life before the end of his life. Since either of the diseases which will ultimately kill him is the sort that gives weeks, more likely months, and possibly even a year or more's notice, before it finally does him in, there is a good chance that he can bring it off.

In Grieben's race against death to finish something which he feels *must* be finished, I am sure you can see certain parallels with my own situation—parallels which by their mere existence (and not because of anyone's knowledge) should add substance or reality to the book. Or so, at least, I hope. . . .

DALTON

Part IV

—◆—

DRAFTS
AND
NOTES

EDITOR'S NOTE

"In the opening chapter," Trumbo wrote to Wilson, "I intend to have him stare at two cardboard cartons held together by ropes, and to realize that those two shabby cartons contain the whole history of his life." Two such cartons contained the manuscript, drafts, notes, and research materials Trumbo had gathered for *Night of the Aurochs*. Most of the material was in the form of research notes on German history and particularly the history of the Nazi period. None of this has been included with the exception of a few sample quotations from Luther and Chekhov, which Trumbo kept in his notes on the writing of the book. Several variant beginnings and endings are here, a long section of fragments which fill out the characterization, biography, and views of Grieben, and finally a section called Random Notes, which are from Trumbo to himself as author. Only those which seemed germane to the story are reprinted. The notes on anti-Semitism and the curious episode of Grieben's obsession about Anne Frank are included as examples.

ALTERNATE BEGINNINGS

I am willing to grant memory, especially in a man of my years, is more errant than the course of a fallen leaf on a windy day. Although a graph of its movement in any given week would describe a pattern of chance too idiotic to explain. If the leaf is real, and for its every mindless movement there is a reason; not a purpose, unless one wants to drag God into the matter, but certainly a reason. Thus understood, the imprint of a single leaf upon the autumn air becomes an exercise in logic as majestic as the endless generation of celestial time. Just so, an old man's memory. For each unsettling disconnection, each wild leap through time and substance, there is a reason, a consistency, a logic of this spirit, which verge more closely on the truth than any possible sequence of sworn to and attested facts.

Why is this? Because without memory there is no way to comprehend the meaning of factual truth, or to put the matter more directly, of reality. The recollection of a rose smelled fifty years ago contains more of objective reality than the most authentic analysis of the perfume that emanates or the chemical elements of which its scent consists. Only in relative terms (the smell of shit being inescapable while that of roses must be pursued) is it possible to describe the fragrance of a rose ("its smell is more agreeable than that of shit") to those who have never smelled one.

◆

Everything that I am putting down in these tablets will be based on memory or the written record. Memory, of course, moves as erratically as a butterfly. Like the flashings of a butterfly, which leaves on the summer air the imprint of an idiot's maze.

Memory, they say, is not the best witness. Perhaps not. One thing, however, I am certain of: no man can describe the fragrance of a rose as vividly as he can remember it.

In the end, a man's life comes down to paper and memory. In my case the paper filled less than two cardboard cartons of the kind that were filled with bottles of dark Bavarian beer.

ALTERNATE ENDINGS

Yes. I know. We killed God. But in killing him we killed a corpse. I bid you goodnight. Sweet dreams. Sleep.

I believe it is all a joke, a monstrous joke. We thought we were killing God, when he was already a corpse. What a joke it really was. We thought we were killing God.

The noblest crime of all of them is deicide. Is not deicide the noblest of all crimes? That was both a dream and a joke. We spent our lives, our blood, and our homes on the impossible task of murdering a God already dead. Belaboring a corpse. (Thus the dream became a joke.) Jews murdered the Son. We set out to murder the Father.

We thought not only to equal the Jews but to excel them. They killed the Son, we would kill the Father. Is not deicide the noblest crime of all? To kill God Himself. In that one instant of life between the void and the void, we sought to kill God.

Israel, oh Israel—here gave I unto thee thy soul—and here thou gavest unto me mine. Here was the unforeseen comforting circle of the imagined universe dissolved into something which has become a straight line—a continuum without beginning and without end—the inconceivable truth of infinity, which God invented, designed, perfected, and made eternal for no better purpose than to drive us mad—and here we stand for all time—the hunter and the hunted—the killer and the killed—confirmed through time and depth and hunger and space beyond dimension and measurement because they never began and cannot end— what we have done here is forever and ever. Amen. Gloria in excelsis.

♦

My virility is to reject. I reject everything by which you live. I see the falseness of it. Realizing it, I hate it. Hating it, I will destroy it. I am the avenging evil. Anything is preferable to the nothing that is you and they. Blood in the veins of yea-saying slaves is no blood at all. It becomes real only when you shed it. Let it flow. Let reality reign.

♦

Are we falling in love again? I do not know. My life is a waste, a scum. There are new flavors here. There is a new kind of death, a death of the spirit, out of which we have created a new nation. Oh Israel, Israel, here gave I unto thee thy soul! The clouds glower, the air grows chill, gray wind through gray, lifeless trees, dead souls in the mist, a moaning, a sigh. Are we falling in love again?

DOG BARKS

Tonight, after listening to the news, I left the house to sit and think and inhale the dry air of a late August night—an atmosphere which to me has always carried the smell of an herb cellar: dry grasses, fallen leaves, pods of parched seeds, a rotted wild cucumber, the cast-off husks of grasshoppers and garter snakes, the hollow corpses of exiled drone bees, the flutter of disconnected moth parts—the whole gaudy corpse of summer decked with shabby flights of mortuary art: a sunflower stalkhead bowed with grief, thorns of a dry locust for the making of crowns, the spear of an infant poplar tree that survived its first season, straight and sharp and deadly, and, far and high to the north, the pole star pointed to the Big Dipper for the convenience of lost children, while nearer at hand a telephone pole stood stark against the horizon for emergency crucifixions. The distant hum of motor traffic could be heard rushing about on errands of absolutely no importance, a sound never heard in my youth. A train whistle announcing from far off the miracle of its determined passsage from Erlangen to Bamberg. The shouts of children, loud and deceptively raucous, save from time to time as they start to disguise suspicious nighttime games with giggles and suppressed laughter. From somewhere near the river came the howling of a dog—just one dog, no more—a tireless howl without change of rhythm or tone or passion or, which is more interesting, response. The mindless boredom of that howl, its dismal monotony, the feeling it conveyed, that one no longer existed in the world but in a state of temporarily violent void, and that the awesome horror of the world is its truth, perhaps the only incontestable truth that neither the human mind nor the cleverest computer can either prove or disprove.

There must be four thousand persons who live in Forchheim. Because it is a rural area, almost everyone in the village and countryside keeps a dog. On an ordinary night several dogs are barking at the same time—a blended chorus of sounds so ordinary, so expected, and not to be consciously heard at all, just as one doesn't hear the singing of crickets. It is simply a rule of nature that dogs bark at night; that occasionally one of them howls; and that there are times when, stirred by some spiritual madness, the whole community of dogs takes to howling en masse. But I had never before known a night when, for the lamentations of one howling dog, the universe gave forth no sound at all.

Old Fritz, who dozed at my feet, twitching and hyperventilating occasionally at the dreamed memory of some ancient canine horror, remained as soundless as the rest. Then, like the crash of thunder heard from on the other side of the world, there was a gunshot. The howling stopped, old Fritz looked up, surveyed the night with rheumy eyes, drew his conclusions, and allowed his head to collapse with a soft thump against the stoop.

Then, now far from the river a Great Dane broke the silence, after which every dog in Forchheim and on all the farms just around it joined the chorus. The crisis was at an end. Even the crickets sounded louder than when the original dog sent forth its first howling lament. I know it was a Great Dane that terminated the weird enchantment of the dogs in Forchheim that night because Gunther's dog was a Great Dane, and the sound of their bark is not to be mistaken.

I picture myself sitting there on my stoop in the darkness, an old man of seventy-one, thinking not of the dry autumnal earth, nor of the gunshot, nor the growing chill as the moon sailed higher, but staring up at the night sky, listening across half a century to the bark of Gunther's Great Dane, and the sound of Gunther whistling it down, and for the sound of Gunther's voice on Hoher Meissner singing side by side with mine on that miraculous star-clustered night that marked both the end of my life and its beginning.

Grieben: Biography

CHRONOLOGY

Events	Grieben's Age
Grieben born, 1898	
Wandervogel in 1913	15
Joins Army, 1916	18
End of War; joins Freikorps	
Freikorps	
Married in 1923 or 1924	25–26
Son born in 1925	27
Joined the Party, 1926	28
Daughter born in 1928	30
Leaves SA, joins SS in 1934	36
Killer unit, Russia, 1941–42	43–44
Auschwitz, 1942	44
Second daughter born, 1944	46
(Note: the baby was killed	
with the mother in Dresden)	
Grieben caught in 1947	
Freed seven years later	
in 1954	

Grieben: Autobiography

Seven stiff cardboard boxes, each firmly bound on all four sides with strong, cheap field rope; three duffel bags of canvas, waterproofed and well protected from all but fire; ten melon boxes for objects that don't require too much protection against the wet. I sit here in my cubicled bedroom at Forchheim and wonder how they packed so much of the damned stuff into it (although I watched them carefully, checked each item against the carbon that should, at least, have rendered full account of them).

The problem, as any kind of fool can see, is autobiography. How is it possible to write about one's self and still tell the truth? Or, just as difficult, even to write truly what one *thinks* to be the truth?

◆

Fairs were much simpler when I was a boy; there were wild horses, of course, and holy dwarfs, and every third female child was christened Ptomane, and when the face of the inviolate morn turned ever so slightly toward the equinox, hundreds of millions of holy elvers swarmed seaward down almost every scenically important European river. They squirmed and jostled and wept, being borne with foreknowledge and therefore understanding how few their survivors would compare to the staggering mass of them who set forth upon that long and perilous journey.

Grieben: Biography

He loves to read American reports about Charles A. Lindbergh, Senator Nye, Father Coughlin, Hearst papers, and the *Chicago Tribune*.

♦

Grieben's parents lost their house and everything during the inflation. By 1924 he is thoroughly declassed.

♦

Grieben gets a job during inflation, hunting out and paying off mortgage holders who are hiding to avoid paying. One of them shoots himself as Grieben closes in on him. He quits.

♦

Grieben has a friend who rises fast in the SS. He envies him—but he has learned many official secrets from him also—Grieben, beautiful failure—his friend, assured success: until the end, where the friend, disgraced, arrives at Auschwitz for execution. Grieben does it.

The man who tipped Grieben off to the coming purge and recruited him into the SS and saved his life—was his closest friend—is the SS man he has to kill at Auschwitz.

♦

The same atom of ergone which quite accidentally left my lungs for Liesel's in our last kiss may itself have drifted across the cheek of Jesus from Judas's last kiss as he suspended in air at this moment and at this moment [. . .] the seeking lips of the foulest whore in [. . .]. Not as *like*, but the same one.

Thus it was that night as I knelt on the hillock in the gray twilight of Auschwitz. The giraffes were grazing. Smoke poured from their ears, and their cheeks glowed red as their teeth ground hot bone to ash. Lifted their heads, regarded the horizons, calmly continued their grazing.

♦

At his trial Grieben is very proud to have referred to the American flag as an "accountant's flag." It is the only flag in the world that changes when a new state is united with the rest of the states. It is a flag that *counts*, enumerates. Hence, it is never permanent, as all other national flags are. It is always temporary. There will be fifty-one, fifty-two, etc., stars.

Grieben: Diary Insert per Russia

It is out at last, the incredible news which we, who were ordered
to assemble in Pretzsch, have known since the second of June:
yesterday at dawn we crossed the frontiers of Communist Russia
on a 2000-mile front, objectives Leningrad in the north, Moscow
in the west, Odessa to the south.

Looking like a newborn child, the map of a Europe that we
have [moot?] never existed before. Of France, including that great
whore of whores which is Paris; Luxembourg, Denmark, Norway,
Finland, Poland, Austria, Czechoslavakia, Yugoslavia, Bulgaria,
Hungary, Rumania, White Russia, the Ukraine, Greece, Albania,
Montenegro, Italy, and North Africa from [. . .] to [. . .].

In the face of all this glory, in the seat of this unparalleled empire, in the midst of all these riches, we now move in an irresistible tide against St. Petersburg's frozen palaces and the golden
domes of Moscow. God be with us.

Grieben: On Women

Women as available everywhere; they are common; man is the greatest quarry, the best of all game. Have him and you have something. Have a woman and you have all of them—they are always there, all to be fucked—man is different.

♦

Grieben's relationship with women somewhat parallels Germany's historical relationship with non-German people. He has always translated love as power, and power is the right to use, misuse, or abuse the beloved as he wishes. Thus, after his great years are over, he realizes with a tragic sense of loss and yearning that never in his life has he been truly loved by a woman.

His childhood venture with Inge degenerated into fantasies of abuse, and she ended hating him. Beata, the plain woman he married because she owned a cottage free and clear and hence was at the peak of German inflation, he never loved nor pretended to. Not loving her, he didn't abuse her; he simply used her as a cow, a household servant, and, when unavoidable, as a sexual obligation to be dealt with as swiftly and brutally as possible.

Leisel, who became the one great love of his life, so successfully avoided his sexual advances that on the night of the great bookburning in the square of Berlin University he took her into the park across from the University and attempted to rape her. However, at the moment of genital contact he prematurely ejaculated, merely soiling her loins. While he tearfully apologizes for what he calls his excess of masculine sexuality she vanishes into the night. Vanishes completely; never returning to the opera, never returning to her apartment. His frantic search and a consequent SS investigation reveal only that she is descended from one Jewish grandmother. Years later when he is a power in Auschwitz, he spots her in the street during a visit to Berlin and he sets the SS on her. He discovers she is married to a professor at the Max Planck Institute and has two young children. He has her kidnapped and brought to Auschwitz, where he arranges to save her from the ovens at the last moment and use her thereafter as his personal slave. She feigns gratitude because she must satisfy every demand he makes of her, and actually pretends to love him in order to survive and ultimately return to her husband and children.

All the horrors of love and sexual abuse which he merely fantasized or played at with Inge became a daily reality with Leisel. Why? Because he loves her so desperately.

When she is inadvertently killed during the evacuation of Auschwitz in the face of the Russian advance, he buries her in the woods near the camp. Only after death, and at the very peak of his terrible grief, he discovers that far from loving him as he thought, she loathed and feared him to a point of hatred. That behind each protestation of love, each kiss, each caress, each act of sweetness and submission, there had been nothing but fear, loathing, and a hatred too terrible to be imagined.

Thus, at fifty-four, having given his whole life to the lost German cause and now rotting in prison for fidelity to his oath, he comes to the terrible realization that he is approaching the end of his life without, even for one fleeting moment, having been truly loved by a woman.

The recognition of this horror arouses in him a terrible hunger for the one experience that justifies human existence and enables man to contemplate the inevitable approach of his own dissolution without going mad.

Let me have one moment, give me one moment. In his black despair he prays to God to grant him for just one moment, for only one fleeting moment, the experience of being loved by a woman.

Thus, in 1952, while in [. . .] Prison, he reads the first German translation of Anne Frank's diary. It infuriates him. He and all his fellow prisoners, and a large section of the German community, denounce it as a Jewish forgery. However, 900,000 copies of the diary are printed in Germany alone, and public opinion changes; and in the diary's wake come other books that not only confirm the diary's validity, but establish that Anne Frank and her entire family arrived at Auschwitz in September 1944.

Knowing now that Anne Frank was a real person, and that for at least three months (until camp evacuation and her transfer to Bergen-Belsen and death), he and fifteen-year-old Anne shared the spiritual and emotional trauma of Auschwitz, breathed the same air, felt the same autumnal chill.

The knowledge that this fifteen-year-old girl actually [. . .], he begins to identify his life with hers. For at least three months, he and this fifteen-year-old girl beheld the same chimneys, looked up at the same smoke-fogged skies, breathed the same air, and inhaled smoke from the same crematory chimneys, shivered with the chill of the same autumnal winds, and dreamed of a future neither could predict or understand.

Since he had frequent [. . .] in the [. . .] area of the camp where the women were employed, it seems likely that he actually saw this girl and that she actually saw him. Even more, it is probable that they actually spoke to each other, and even in some curious way came to *know* each other.

With the ascendance of Dr. [. . .] and others, he spends the rest of his prison term learning everything about Auschwitz in the last four months of 1944. It was not difficult to get research material, since the conditions of imprisonment for people like Grieben were far from severe.

♦

Every man can have a woman—many women can have a woman—but to have had a *man!* That no woman has ever had.

Grieben: On Conscience

There were, even in my circumstances, moments of clarity, instants of illumination, those strange split-seconds of time when all is seen, observed, analyzed—and nothing is understood. It is there, no question about that. The light reveals it. The eye sees it. But the spirit, the mind, the conscience of man—whatever you want to call it—turns blind and will not see it. It will not see because it cannot and still live. I mean, live in the same way, by the same right. That is because the right is from a different world and that world we dare not enter without abandoning ourselves. I speak of the world of anti-matter, of the anti-world, that positive negation, which scientists say is so complicated and mysterious that it cannot be understood; but of course when they say that to us, they are lying. They see, and they understand perfectly, and they deny it because they fear it. He was no fool who urged us not to bring the Visigoths to save us from the Scythians.

Grieben: On Leadership

The search for leadership is the search for *love*. Someone to love, to trust, to obey, to die for. If there is nothing to die for, there is nothing to live for. To live for, so intensely, so all consumingly that it is the apotheosis of life and love. We walk from the day we are born toward the past, toward the night, toward extinction, toward the nothingness whence we came. I see there is no purpose but to be, but to act, but to declare life everywhere and in every form before we go out.

Grieben: On Leadership and Death

Toward the end do they not realize that our innocent young boys died on our side too? Curse the leadership on both sides. Damn the generals and kings and presidents on both sides. Curse them, curse me! My mother! curse her private parts that they did not strangle me at birth! Curse God—the world—life—the dead are all innocent! Can't you understand that? They are paid by the millions! Let me join them in their wormy dust!

Grieben: On Power

List of Grieben's power relationships. Power:

> Over squirrel
> Over rabbit
> Over Inge
> Over Liesel
> Over Gunther
> Over farmer
> Over wife

Grieben: On Germany

Here we were, a few tens of millions of Germans, the gathering together of all the Teutonic tribes, surrounded by the intolerable pressure of earth's hundreds of millions, a world overflowing with enemies, hating us, envying us, wanting to trick us, to trample us into the mire as they had in the past—not a people but a folk, a family, a tribe, blood brothers together, living in this beautiful German land, these haunted German forests, these ordered German fields, these rivers, these lakes, these waters and marshes bounded by gray seas, these bitter shores.

◆

In these days, or years, there arose from every point of Germany's pulsing heart what became known as the Y.M. (Youth Movement), a time when the very best of German youth took to the roads and fields, the rivers and trails, to the forests and mountaintops in search of—of what? Of ourselves, really; of our *true* selves; of something beyond ourselves, something larger than the loneliness of the individual; a search, in short, for brotherhood and for fatherhood—a true father, a leader, a Christ, a Messiah, a Wotan, if you wish—someone whom we could trust and love and follow; someone to whom in perfect faith and love we could surrender ourselves and our lives in a moment of communion when he surrendered himself and his life to us.

♦

There is a loneliness at the heart of the German mystery—a loneliness that springs from—

You don't know us, you of the outer world, you don't understand us for what we are and you never have. You don't know us because you look at us as Germans, whereas we look at ourselves as the German folk, which is something altogether different. You understand neither us nor our loneliness.

Here we were, a few tens of millions of Germans, the gathering together of all the Teutonic tribes, surrounded by the intolerable pressure of earth's hundreds of millions, a world overflowing with enemies, hating us, envying us, wanting to trick us, to trample us into the mire as they had in the past—not the people but a folk, a family, a tribe, blood brothers together, living in this beautiful German land, these haunted German forests, these ordered German fields, these rivers, these lakes, these waters and marshes bounded by the gray seas, these bitter shores.

Grieben: On German Gods and History

These were our Gods before Christianity—and we knew they had died because the old Norse were the only people on earth who had Gods they knew would die. To worship a mortal God is to be thrown back on oneself as we were and are, and yet be a Christian.

We of the North had no such sunny expectations. We knew that the Gods we worshipped—Woden, Thor, Tiw and their blood kin and allies—were constantly beset by treachery of enemies as strong as they, and which [. . .] we knew that one day the enemies would triumph—in Icelandic, the term is *Ragnarok*: "The fatal destiny, end of the Gods"—and that our gods would die. It is one thing to worship Gods who could not possibly die, or fail, or be overthrown or cast aside or in any way brought low; it requires an entirely different kind of man, sterner, stronger, and infinitely more tough-minded, the stake of destiny of a whole people on the service and worship of Gods who were, like the worshippers themselves, doomed to mortality and death. Where is the profit in worshipping Gods who cannot save themselves from death, much less their followers? That, of course, is the point of the whole matter. There was no profit, or any expectation of it: the Western commercial concept that worship is something to be rewarded is utterly, absolutely incomprehensible to anyone of German birth or blood or soul. In matters spiritual we have always preferred to give rather than to take. It is for this reason, perhaps, that our Western friends have so often charged us with savagery.

Who but a savage would worship rather than bargain with his Gods?

Twenty years of war, in the course of which hunger alone diminished the height of a single generation by half an inch; the War of the League of Angsling, which lasted nine years; the twelve-year War of the Spanish Succession followed by the first Northern War, which lasted five years and the Second, which lasted twenty. Then, beginning with the war of the Polish Succession, a quarter century of warfare, which included the Silesian War, the War of the Austrian Succession, and the Seven Years' War, after which the Napoleonic Wars tormented Europe, but primarily the Germans from 1792 to 1814.

Thus, in the 196 years between the Defenestration of Prague in 1618 and the final deposition of Napoleon in 1814, the German people endured 123 years of war, raping, invasion, occupation, pillage, dismemberment, defeat.

For over two centuries and far into a third, their central position in Europe had made German lands the tramping ground of Europe and the [. . .] point between Roman West and Byzantine East a mere transit area for all the armies of Europe.

What made it even more horrible is that there seemed no way out. During the centuries of German torment, Britain, France, Spain, Sweden, Russia, and even tiny Denmark had become nations, each a unified people with a central government and a historical identity, while we, the Germans, remained a segment and collection of kingdoms, grand duchies, principalities, free cities, and leagues of cities—in short, a concourse of medieval states and fiefs as out of place in the nineteenth century as, let us say, Afghanistan in the twentieth century.

Not until 1870 was there truly a German state, but even then, forty-three years later, in 1913, it was a Germany with four regnant kings, five grand duchies, and thirteen duchies and principalities, all with their separate courts and ruling parties, ranking in power and glory from Wilhelm II, the King of Prussia and German Emperor, to his Serene Highness the Count Regent of Lippe-Detmold.

Grieben: On Wandervoegel

What no one understood about those thousands of campfires that winked like stars from the crest of Hoher Meissner during the warm July nights of 1913—indeed, what no non-German has ever understood about the German people themselves—is the loneliness, the lovingness, the longing, the overwhelming melancholy the campfires symbolized, which the true German has felt in his heart since the beginning of time.

Of all the world's great peoples, we alone, Teuton, Nordic, Aryans—call us what you will—and from the very beginnings of our history, did not believe the world would endure forever, or that the gods were immortal. Other ancient peoples—the Egyptians, the Persians, the Greeks, and the Romans—had pursued their racial and national destinies under the rule and patronage and laws of immortal gods whose dominion would endure, as would they themselves, until all eternity.

Grieben: On Religion

Don't talk to me about God or Jesus or faith or religion. I appeal to God only with exclamation points, I cry out to Jesus from an excess of bad temper, but I do it only because I am lonely and I know they aren't there anyhow. If they were there I would maintain perfect silence and so would everyone else, because only a fool would expose himself.

But they aren't there, and they never were there, and they never will be. We are taught to believe in them (or else we invent them for ourselves) because we are all so milk-minded that we can't face up to the simple truths of a world and an existence without them. We loathe or fear ourselves so terribly we simply can't believe that we alone are the only help we shall ever have. Bishops, cardinals, popes, prophets, shamans, lamas, gurus, and muezzins daily and newly bewitch themselves and the world. Look at the scientists, for God's sake, observe them carefully as they contemplate the idea of an infinity that drives them insane because it doesn't conform to what they know about their own measurable lives—that they are conceived, are born, grow old, wear out, and finally cease to exist. To straighten matters out and soothe their quivering bowels at three o'clock in the morning they dream like imaginative children or Old Testament prophets of a universe that began as precise but imprecisely known into the eternal time that will end at a time equally precise but just as imprecisely known.

What are they looking for when they project a universe that began with a cosmic bang, expanded to outer reaches so distant that they can't even be imagined by man, and will end, like Saint John's great gathering of souls, in a cosmic collapse as its elements rush back upon themselves to borrow what they were before the universe began?

They are searching for an act of creation, aren't they? Of course! They are searching for the moment when the universe and everything that is or ever was in it came into being, for the means by which it came into being, and for the power that activated those means. They are searching, in short, for the God who created this universe, and nothing less will satisfy them. Instead of the Old Testament God who created all in seven days they are searching for a new God, a force, who created all with a big bang. Is the first God more a product of superstition or less philosphically believable and satisfying than the second?

Not at all. Why not? Because the God-created universe of Genesis and the bang-created universe of modern science derive from the most primitive of all man's superstitions—that there *was* a beginning and hence that there can be an end.

Because there isn't. There is neither beginning nor end to truth, to infinity, to eternity, to the universe. That is the Genesis and the bang-created universe of modern astrophysics derive from the most comforting of man's primitive superstitions—that there was a beginning, a marvelous act of creation that caused the universe to become, hence that there can be an end of Genesis and the bang-created universe of modern astrophysics, both derive from man's most primitive and comforting superstition—that the universe began with a marvelous act of creation that will end in apocalypse.

But despite the prayers of scientists and the best calculations of theologians it isn't true. The fact that the universe never began deprives them of their creative act. The fact that what never began can never end deprives them of surrender's sweetest consolation. Thus, for endless generations. . . .

Grieben: The Ultimate Horror
of My Life

The ultimate horror which my life and my sufferings and the sufferings of others have taught me.

Because it isn't. The universe never began because it has no beginning, and because it has no beginning it can have no end—it is eternal. It is infinite. It is completely without dimension. That is why good theologians and our theology have told billions of solemn, mindless, lonely, frightened idiots that there is something divine out there that has meaning. If you told them it isn't there and never was there, they would go mad.

Look at the scientists, for God's sake. Observe them carefully as they dance like dervishes in maniacal search for a neat little beginning of the universe and rounded off by a neat little end.

But it isn't there. Despite the prayers of scientists and the cunning miscalculations of theologians, the creative act of beginning for which they search never was, and the merciful act of final destruction, the hope of which they are inconsolable can never be. They are left only with that which they will not see—the shuddering horror of a universe both eternal and infinite without beginning, without end, without dimension, without time, without hope.

The cosmic bang will end as a vast inward cosmic collapse on itself. One theory is that the universe curves in upon itself and that beyond the curve there is nothing.

The terror of a void is not that it is nothing but that it is *something*. It is real and—unendurable.

Grieben: On Killing and Guilt

You killed the Greeks. You killed the Armenians. You killed the Huguenots. You killed the Protestants. You killed the Catholics. You killed the Gypsies. You killed the Poles. You killed the Ukrainians. You killed the Indians and the Malaysians and the Ceylonese. You killed the Bantu and the Riff and the Egyptians and Arabians and the Indonesians and the (here we shall add a large number of Colonial peoples who were killed during the eighteenth and nineteenth centuries).

And what have we done? We have killed a handful of Jews, for Christ's sake—and a handful the world wanted to get rid of in any event.

God in heaven, is it all guilt? everywhere? we know there is guilt in hell. We know that day in and out we sweat beneath the burden of our intolerable guilt on earth. Is it possible then, that there is no guilt in heaven also? Ah yes, of course. There is guilt everywhere and there is repentance everywhere, but where is there forgiveness? I think there must have been a moment in time whilst I, pale as a grub and insatiably greedy for the rotting red flesh of my mother's womb, caught my first wish of guilt without sin, of sin without repentance, and of repentance without forgiveness. And in that moment of larval cannibalism I reached, without knowing it, the conclusion which inevitably was to govern my life: Fuck it; fuck it all. If I am not to be forgiven then I shall not repent.

Grieben: On Killing and the Camps

Most of them drink but I resist the temptation. I will not make it easy. I will take the full burden of guilt.

♦

Effect of Concentration Camp Work on the Sexual Drive of the Personnel. If the sexual drive constitutes an essential or even an important part of man's psyche, the effect of our work in Auschwitz was almost as crippling to us of the SS as to the unnumbered tens of thousands of females who passed each week from our custody into God's. To this today [...] misbegotten travel agents have caused them to pay good money for a "guided tour" through Eastern Poland—a tour to what remains of the great encampment between the waters of [...] and the [...] rivers are now labeled on the map, but once properly called Auschwitz or Auschwitz-Birkenau, are exhibited as lovingly as remains of the Imperial Forum by the Romans or the eternally silent pink facades of Petra by those degenerate heirs of what we once [...]. Let those who pass through the narrow streets and still well-stuffed warehouses of Auschwitz remember that here a thousand troopers of the SS sacrificed their natural instincts, their innate capacities for ...

(The idea of nude women as meat in transit—and what it is like to SS personnel—the sexual appetite can no longer be stimulated by the old means—the nude female body, for example. It calls for new and different stimuli, or else it dies altogether, or turns sick, perverse, corrupt.)

♦

I have no humanity in me.

Grieben: The Camp

In dark moments he hears the music of the camp orchestra. One night in Forchheim, it awakens him. He knows something is wrong. The orchestra *never* plays at night, because night shipments are always held in the train cars until morning. He gets up, goes out in his nightshirt, stares into the quiet night. Yes. They're playing, all right. Over there. On the verge of the forest, the Jews are playing Mozart! He sits down on his step, listens. When the piece is ended and silence comes to the scene, he sighs, arises, and goes back to bed.

Grieben: On the Jews

The intense desire for nationhood which animated the Nazis produced in their Jewish victims, who had never yearned for it, their own drive for nationhood.

♦

The personnel (Jewish) who mysteriously challenge him, even before the prisoner himself is aware that Grieben *feels* challenged. Grieben seeks him out (indirectly), manipulates him. Prisoner unaware. Grieben cannot believe the man's nobility, cannot believe he is a Jew. Makes elaborate checks into his ancestry (all of which, naturally, prolong the prisoner's life). The man *is* a Jew. All the way a Jew. To corrupt the prisoner, of which the prisoner is totally unaware. At the very end, he *does* corrupt the prisoner. His rage, his anguish, his terrible disillusionment.

He charges prisoner: the mutual recognition: something terrible emotional and moral [. . .]: sends prisoner to his death. Prisoner has betrayed far more than he, Grieben, has.

I do not understand these people, and because I do not understand them I kill them. Oh God, how I hate these somber-eyed, accommodating, acquiescing Jews! How meekly they walk to their deaths. Nietzsche was no fool when he wrote of the terrible meek, and their meekness shames death itself. Reduces death's messengers to the status of clerks, of [...]. I hate these somber-eyed, accommodating, acquiescing Jews who walk so meekly to their deaths. Their acquiescence denies you combat, denies you struggle, and when they descend at last into the common ground they take not only your honor with them but your humanity as well.

On order they dig their graves, strip off their clothes, march to the killing place.

Birth, through accidental coincidence of concupiscence with ovulation, is the gift of man; death is the gift of God, and to ridicule death by acquiescence is to make a fool of God himself.

There is no accounting for these Jews. You threaten them, they yield; you order them out of your country, they dig in silently, sullenly, tenaciously, remain; you tell them that if they don't go you will throw them in jail, they remain and go threateningly, terrifyingly to jail; you tell them you will kill them, they defy you to kill them; you tell them to march to their deaths, they march to their deaths; you tell them to dig their graves, they dig their graves; you tell them to undress on the brink of their graves, they undress on the brink of their graves; you tell them to stand for the death blow, they stand for the death blow; you tell them you are going to kill them, they force you to kill them; and while they so arrogantly, so carelessly degrade you to animals, they deny you combat, deny you the struggle, deny you your soldier's function and purpose, they deny you the right to combat; and when they descend into their graves they take not only your soldier's honor but your manhood and even your humanity with them. Nietzsche was no fool when he wrote of the terrible meek; their meekness defies death itself and reduces death's messengers to the status of ribbon clerks and delivery boys, is to reduce God to a mindless idiot.

I hate these accommodating, acquiescing Jews. When they walk so meekly to their deaths there is no dignity left over for their executions. By acquiescence they degraded us all.... What a horrible, aggressive, terrible ferocity is their acquiescence! They cannot be human because if they were we, too, would share in their acquiescence, and this no man could do and still remain a man.

On they come, naked as children, skinny old men with beards, women with thick legs and stout, rolling menopausal haunches, mothers with huddled, bare-skinned children, limp-penised fathers shamed by their helplessness, boys white as newly dug grubs, girls in bud with huge eyes, if right-handed, covering their genitals with the left, and if left-handed, with the right, others enfolding their tough little breasts—and looking at us—all of them looking at us as if we weren't there—or if there, not human—as if we were beasts—not recognizing that we, like them, are under orders; that we, like them, only obey or die; that we, like them, are *also* human beings.

Why do they yield like this? Why do they drag us down? Why do they [. . .]?

Grieben: On Anti-Semitism

Grieben realizes that in embracing anti-Semitism he has forsaken Germania and accepted *Christianity*!!!

◆

It amazes him when the haughty, anti-Semitic (i.e., anti-Eastern) Jews of Germany discover their fate to be no different from the Jews they hold in such contempt. *Important.* Grieben exults over this because German Jews, in their contempt for and characterizations of Eastern Jews, have defined and subscribed to the views of anti-Semitism which will soon be applied to them.

Grieben: On Old Age

The idiot who called old age "the golden years" was full of shit. They are the lonely years, the regretful years, and if one is lucky, as I consider myself to be, they are filled almost daily with previously undiscovered little pains. For the unlucky ones the pains grow into an agony of the mind and body that reduces them to blabbering, bed-shitting constructions of bone and gristle and scaling skin. I would gladly give up these golden years tomorrow, did it not take so much longer than I had calculated to set down these notes about my life and what it has meant to me and others. I am determined not to until the task I so foolishly set for myself is finished. "Who do you think will read it?" I ask myself. "No one," I answer. "Then why?" "Because I was here," I tell myself. "I was once an inhabitant of this earth, and that is a fact that should be recorded. A record must be made. Also explanations, even if they are made only to myself."

I used to have my shepherd dog Fritz to while away the hours with me—particularly the night hours. It was a good feeling to feel the warmth of his body as it lay sleeping on the quilt at the foot of my bed. But I was too kind to him. I fed him too much, and he grew fat and one morning I found his body on the quilt stiff in death.

I buried him in the woods as I had buried Liesel so many years before, and occasionally I take a flower to his grave. However I soon discovered that I could not bear life without something that was also alive around the house. It had to be a dog, of course, because I am not at all fond of cats. Also, since my increasing frailty made it difficult to hold the leash on a dog of Fritz's size, I purchased a three-month-old dachshund pup, which I named Willy. Although he had all the charm of a mournful clown, both of us were too old for efficient training. The warmth of his small body against my feet at night was of course the purest pleasure, which I tolerated despite the fact that for all my watchfulness, he deposited his dung where he wished, pissed dutifully and copiously wherever old Fritz's scent was strongest, and could not be prevented from running out into the street. Finally, for his own good as well as mine.

Grieben: On Dying

The plain truth is that I am dying. First the excision, at age seventy-four, of a cancerous left lung. Then the heart attack. And finally, after many tests, the diagnosis of chronic corpulmonale, which in my case is progressive and not subject to arrest or cure.

Six months after the surgeon's knife first had its way with me, I could walk a slow mile with moments out for rest without too much difficulty in breathing. Today, a year and a half after surgery, I cannot move from bedroom to front-door stoop without panting like a dog. That is a measure of the rate of deterioration which has set in and will continue.

A year from now, or perhaps sooner, I shall be dead. Since the cancer has given no signals of metastasis, I can even look forward to a fairly easier but earlier death: a heart attack, which is quick and merciful, or the slower but not too agonizing process of pneumonic strangulation caused by a tired heart's inability to clear the body of liquid waste. Considering that every man must die of something, my death at the age of seventy-six or seventy-seven will not be a bad one nor certainly premature.

Grieben: Views

What Grieben must finally realize is from Sartre:

1. There is no redemption for evil.
2. The ultimate and only freedom is the right to say "No" and die for it. Man's freedom is to say, "No!"

I shall continue to be as dust, creative, organic matter and thus am comfortable because I shall mulch new life and live in it. No. There is no comfort because it is not true! I shall die and be nothing! Therefore, why did I live? Or *did* I? Was I nothing from the moment of my birth? Yes! There's the horror!

I am a copulating vegetable. Shake the carrots together in a sack and their passion is just as great as mine.

Through Sartre:—that man is an alien in the universe, unjustified and unjustifiable; there is no reason sufficient to explain why man or his universe exists. No purpose. No goal. Death is life. Life is death. Let them die. *There was actually a better reason for killing them—or any other group of people—than for rescuing them.*

◆

As a child I always felt secure. I was glad to be what I am. I would lie in my bed before going to sleep, and in those moments just before rising to the magical realm of the unconscious, my mind would wander the world to marvel at the luck which had made of me *me* against such terrible odds. But for chance I could have been an African child, a Mongolian, an American, an Aborigine, even English. But that I had been born white, a German, a Franconian, that I had been born in this particular town in this precise house of these very particular parents—the odds against it were too enormous to be believed. Yet there I was, blessed beyond the mind's wildest dreams, safe, secure, confident, ready to approach even the terrors of sleep with a sense of well-being that comes only to gods. Or so I thought.

◆

Although armies may be maneuvered into war by cunning and hostile statesmen for monetary or other reasons, the armies fight well only for what strikes them as moral or spiritual reasons. When the leaders take their departure from the battlefield (which is what defeat means) so does the soldier's moral and spiritual passion send him off in close pursuit of his betters. The great man wages war for reasons of state: the little man follows and fights only for reasons of passion.

◆

He wants not to give himself to those he loves, but to rule over them, possess them, and the only true way to evidence possession is abuse.

◆

We stumble into our graves knowing so well how to have done better.

◆

One of the curious things about survivors is that to the last man each of them felt that he survived through merit because he deserved to survive.

◆

Death is sleep without knowledge of the pleasure of life.

◆

His conviction that in the end peace, order, prosperity, full employment will drive the world mad with boredom—and that they will rise up finally against it.

◆

The worst criminals on earth are those who toy with love.

◆

The intensity of his love for young girls as he grows very old. He regrets—*really*—that he didn't take every young girl he ever saw—he who had so many opportunities for seduction or rape.

◆

Grieben: "The generals are fat! Only the foot soldiers are slim."

◆

I am trying to penetrate the mystery of why I am as I am—what I am—I have done everything well and right—and it *can't* be wrong because it was right.

◆

With me the problem has always been one of belief. By that I mean that I cannot live without believing in something more important than myself. God is too remote for my need. My whole life has been lived in present time.

From the day I was born I have watched present time become

past, and God, who lives in time future, has shown no interest. I reciprocate.

♦

Don't worry about the skies. There is nobody out there. You are alone. You are alone in the universe. Stop looking. (And here you are all alone.)

♦

There are two great hatreds men are heir to: the hate of life and the hate of death. The first leads to death, the second to life.

♦

I come of a race that scooped its grandmother's brains out with a jagged stone spoon and ate them in the glow of the northern lights.

♦

The child tortures the fly because he has the power to do so, and had not yet learned how mercifully to kill.

♦

The sense of rising again to world leadership, which must be apparent in latter sections of book. We are on the march again, with arms our eternal enemies have given us as allies. This time we shall not fail, for we are the leader of Europe—something we never were before. We are first on the Continent, hence we shall be first in the world. This is a totally new situation.

Trumbo: Note for Novel

Our man considers the Romans—the chief civilizing influence of their day—in relation to Daniel P. Mannix's book called *Those About to Die*. The point that he makes is simply this: The Romans were no less cruel than the Nazis, no less inhuman in their amusements and in their terrible vengeance against certain classes and kinds of people. Yet the Romans were also a highly civilized and cultivated people. Just so were the Germans under the Nazis a highly cultivated and highly civilized people. The point he is making is that a man or a nation does not have to be insane to give way to this human impulse for mass murder. This idea of the insanity of Hitler and of his henchmen is an idea that our narrator wishes to kill. It is also an idea that must be killed. The fact is, of course, that most of the Nazi leaders were perfectly sane. They were giving vent to passions that are felt by all kinds of men all over the world.

Is it absolutely true that culture and science can progress only under conditions of individual freedom? This is a point often made in democratic societies—that the inquiring scientific mind must lie in a climate of intellectual freedom. Yet it is probably not true. Art, science, and culture have flourished under despotisms as well as under democracies. Does anyone, for example, feel that Soviet scientists for the past fifteen years have enjoyed that "climate of intellectual freedom," which we assert exists in Western society? Yet they have made great strides forward, in some ways even surpassing Western society. We must reevaluate this cliché because if it is not exploded we shall never understand the meaning of freedom or of intellectual independence. Perhaps the truest freedom is that in which the individual declares his own mind to be free and clings to that freedom in spite of the exterior restraints of state and society. But if we assert that intellectual achievement is possible only under the circumstances of freedom as freedom is undertood in the West, then we shall be compelled to believe that they are impossible in Russia and in the East. We shall, in other words, be compelled to believe an untruth. If we truly believe what we say, then we shall never be concerned about the achievements of the East because we have already proved they cannot exist, since the circumstances favorable to their growth do not exist. In this way do men deceive themselves by setting forth a philosophical principle, then curiously declining to examine the realities by which the principle can be tested. This is another thing that our man is interested in. He is, in fact, simply trying to prove that the Nazis were perfectly normal intelligent people, and what they did had occurred previously in other societies and times—in nations that were leading the world at the very time they were engaging in the most bestial crimes.

Virtue, given absolute power and if it ever has been given absolute power, has never produced a society which is virtuous. The power of evil when it is absolute has always been able to produce evil unvaryingly and constantly.

We have Angus Cameron's point: All of the progress of the world has been made in a society which, by definition of good and evil, is evil, or at least is not virtuous since a virtuous society has never achieved the ascendency of power. Might it not be that the reason is that a virtuous society never seeks power—that power itself is evil?

Now the point of this is simply as follows: Everything that man has done in this perpetual progress course toward something better has always been done in the midst of savagery, savage societies, and terrible inequities. It would not necessarily follow that the conditions of progress as previously observed are conditions for further progress if we get rid of the savagery.

Our hero Grieben has in the course of his life three male friends. The first one is blinded in the closing phase of World War I. The second one becomes a male prostitute in Berlin in 1925. And the third one Grieben betrays to the SS on the Night of the Long Knives in 1934. After that he really has no male friends. He is actually afraid to have any.

Grieben: A Real-Life Novel

Listen for a moment to a voice which is not Grieben's. It is the voice of Rudolf Hoess, SS commandant of Auschwitz-Birkenau from the beginning of its construction in 1941 to the day of its evacuation in January, 1945:

I . . . see now that the extermination of the Jews was fundamentally wrong. Precisely because of these mass exterminations Germany has drawn upon herself the hatred of the entire world. *It in no way served the cause of anti-Semitism, but on the contrary brought the Jews closer to their ultimate objective.*

My life is now clearly at its end. I have given an account here of everything that was important in that life, all of those things that impressed me most strongly and affected me most deeply. . . . I have described myself as I was and as I am. I have led a full and varied life. I have followed my star wherever it led me. Life has given me some hard and rough knocks, but I have always managed to get along. I have never given in.

My unalterable love for my country brought me into the NSDAP and the SS. I regarded the National Socialist attitude to the world as the only one suited to the German people. I believed that the SS was the most energetic champion of this attitude and that the SS alone was capable of bringing the German people back to its proper way of life.

I remain, as I have always been, a convinced National Socialist in my attitude toward life. When a man has adhered to a belief and an attitude for nigh on twenty-five years, has grown up with it and been bound to it body and soul, he cannot simply throw it away ... I, at least, cannot.

Let the public continue to regard me as the bloodthirsty beast, the cruel sadist, and the mass murderer; for the masses could never imagine the commandant of Auschwitz in any other light. They could never understand that he, too, had a heart and that he was not evil.

Random Notes

I sat last night on my front stoop making designs with the tip of my cane. I did it without looking at the earth as really not paying the slightest attention to what I was doing. Actually, I was looking up into the stars. Depths of the depths of them, great powder-sprinkled vulva receding forever, yet the whole of them is so near that one could bathe in the stars and float on them.

Use this as a lead-in to seduction on Hoher Meissner. The design of the whole is vulvaform (find the words).

This is its literary form, its visual form, its psychological form. Vulvaform represents the seduction of Gunther after the wrestling. Beauty here, poetry, tears, love—and always the receding infinity of the vulva-formed galaxies as the old man thinks and remembers.

Devise execution of Gunther at Auschwitz—as it is discerned in others. Other notes about [. . .].

Old man on front stoop—dreaming in starlight, dreaming of the night on Hoher Meissner—the *vulvaform* shape of the galaxies are equated with Gunther's [. . .]s.

♦

Do not fall into the pit of characterizing "German people." It is always false, always dangerous, and always wicked.

I must make certain to account for the postwar generation in the 1960's.

♦

Grieben hates killing, he constantly tries to escape it, and constantly kills more. He concludes that the whole world's hostility to Jews (and the rejection of them) has compelled Germany (and himself) to accomplish the task which they all wanted to be carried through.

♦

He was in the socialist wing of the SA. Then he saw that there must be an elite of brotherhood leading to a mass of volk [. . .] like Sparta. This is a totally new situation.

♦

"I do not admit that my doctrine can be judged by everyone, even by the angels."—Martin Luther.

♦

"As the ass will have blows, so the mass can be ruled by force."—Martin Luther.

♦

Dig beneath the surface of human character and you will come up with something ugly, be sure of it.

♦

"Man will become better when you show him what it is like."—Chekhov.

♦

The Freikorps: "I want the fight, and man naked and un-ashamed with his sword in his hand; and behind the stars sweeping westward, and before the wind in the grass. It is enough, brothers. [. . .] the word is spoken."

♦

Is this the story of man's return to *humanity?*
"If I had to do it over again"—*what* would he have done?

♦

Oh dear God, don't drabble it out like this. Let me have it in one big lump.

DALTON TRUMBO was the most famous member of "The Hollywood Ten," film writers blacklisted during the McCarthy era. He was born in Montrose, Colorado, on December 9, 1905, and although he later became one of the highest paid screenwriters in Hollywood, his social conscience dominated his life and his work.

His books include the great anti-war novel *Johnny Got His Gun* (1939), which won a National Book Award, and *Additional Dialogue* (1970). His credits as a screenwriter include *A Man to Remember, Kitty Foyle, Thirty Seconds Over Tokyo, The Brave One* (for which he won an Academy Award under the name Robert Rich), *Spartacus, Exodus, Lonely Are the Brave, The Fixer* and *Papillon.* For his screenplay and direction of the movie *Johnny Got His Gun*, he received the International Film Critics Award and the Special Award from the Cannes Film Festival.

Long a fighter against censorship and for trade union rights, Trumbo was a member of the Communist Party from 1943 to 1948. In 1947 he refused to answer questions before the House Un-American Activities Committee and was jailed. From 1947 to 1960 he was blacklisted in Hollywood and went into self-exile in Mexico where he wrote screenplays under numerous pseudonyms. In 1960, Otto Preminger publicly announced he had hired Mr. Trumbo to do the screenplay for *Exodus*, and the blacklisting was broken. Dalton Trumbo died in 1976. He is survived by his wife, Cleo, and three children.

LOON LAKE

by E.L. Doctorow

bestselling author of RAGTIME

(#20027-5 · $3.50)

Distinguished works of fiction,
now in new editions from

BANTAM WINDSTONE BOOKS

THE CONFESSIONS OF NAT TURNER *by William Styron* (#14668-8 • $3.95)
This Pulitzer Prize-winning novel by the author of SOPHIE'S CHOICE is the brilliant story of an American slave revolt led by a remarkable preacher named Nat Turner. *The New York Times* called this novel "magnificent . . . one of those rare books that shows us our American past, our present—ourselves—in a dazzling shaft of light."

GILES GOAT-BOY *by John Barth* (#14705-6 • $4.95)
This bawdy, wickedly funny novel by the author *The New York Times* calls "the best writer of fiction we have in America" features the incredible George Giles, conceived of by a computer, born of a virgin and reared on a goat farm among bucks and does.

NIGHT OF THE AUROCHS *by Dalton Trumbo* (#13919-3 • $3.95)
This gripping final masterpiece by the author of JOHNNY GOT HIS GUN examines the Holocaust from the point of view of the executioner and discovers "that dark yearning for power that lurks in all of us . . . the exquisite perversion when power becomes absolute."

VISION QUEST *by Terry Davis* (#14815-X • $2.50)
This exciting novel by a major new voice in American fiction is at once exuberant and grave, funny and gentle. It has been called by John Irving "the truest novel about growing up since THE CATCHER IN THE RYE."

Read all of these Bantam Windstone Books, available where-paperbacks are sold.